MR JOLLY

Michael Stewart was born in Salford in 1971. His debut novel *King Crow* (Bluemoose, 2011) won *The Guardian*'s 'Not the Booker' Prize, and was the only debut selected as a 'recommended read' for World Book Night 2012. Subsequent publications have included short, themed poetry collection *Couples* (Valley Press, 2013) and a second novel, *Café Assassin* (Bluemoose, 2015).

Michael is senior lecturer in Creative Writing at the University of Huddersfield, and editor of the celebrated series of Grist anthologies. He lives with his partner and son in Bradford.

MR JOLLY

short stories

MICHAEL STEWART

Valley Press

First published in 2016 by Valley Press
Woodend, The Crescent, Scarborough, YO11 2PW
www.valleypressuk.com

ISBN 978-1-908853-60-8
Cat. no. VP0072

Cover and text design by Jamie McGarry
Cover photograph by CGPGrey.com

www.valleypressuk.com/authors/michaelstewart

Supported using public funding by
ARTS COUNCIL
ENGLAND

CONTENTS

for Lisa and Carter

THE LEAGUE

The bald men are gathering outside my gate. I can hear the hum of their voices drifting up through the thin night air. And now I am afraid. Really afraid.

All the fears I have harboured these two score years seem to me now as illusory – my fear of tranquilisers, the prospect of developing Alzheimer's, people with small eyes, ornamental dolls, being in the spotlight, swimming in water which isn't completely clear, beetroot, being a disappointment to those I cherish, ventriloquists, team-building exercises, dead fish – now seem to be mere baubles rather than real fears, irrational anxieties indicative of an over-sensitive personality. As the mob coalesces, I see my genealogy as a chain of phobias passed from one generation to the next like a negatively charged lepton.

I peep through the blinds hanging from the sash window. The tallest bald-head amongst them wields a large crowfoot wrench; a curious armament, but one perhaps reached for in haste. I hear his voice above the crowd: I'm not waiting out here all night, he says.

The men sway and jostle like cattle at a milking shed. Some are armed with makeshift objects of harm: hammers, spanners, gardening tools.

There's a pause before a paunched man wearing shorts offers a rejoinder. What are you suggesting?

Look, we either do nothing or we do something, right? And I know what side of that I'm on.

That seems to be enough to galvanise the herd. Their voices are raised again – shouting, bickering. Someone throws a stone which ricochets off the roofing slates and comes perilously close to the sill of my window. Another raises his fist, accidentally knocking a man's tartan cap off, revealing his pink and smooth pate. Both back and front doors are locked and triple-bolted. The attic door has an inside lock, but it's generic and at best will only stall them. I think about the burlier-framed amongst them shouldering their way into my enclave.

My garret houses a number of packing cases, loaded with books and magazines, carefully categorised. I begin to stack them up against the door. There's sixteen in total and they appear to teeter as the pile gets higher. This will give me a few minutes at most. As I back away from the stacked-up cases, the top pane of the sash window shatters and half a house brick pelts a trajectory across the room, narrowly missing my head and scarring the plaster on the back wall.

I sidle across to the window and peek out from the blinds once more. Things are getting uglier. There must be about thirty or so bald-headed men gathered outside my gate. The tall one who had talked about doing something opens the latch, walks up my pathway and disappears as he approaches my front door. Five of the bald men follow him. I can hear knocking on the door now, first hard, then insistent. Then banging. I hear the letterbox flap open and his voice travel up the stairs.

We know you're in there. You might as well come out, he shouts.

There's a long pause while he waits for a response, and then adds: if you don't come to us, we're going to come to you. Another long pause. I can hear the noise build again and then I hear the door being shoved by what I assume is a bald man's globed shoulder. It won't take him long, I think. The oak door must be over thirty years old, and despite the extra bolts top and bottom, I believe it will give. The battering has become persistent. I search around the room for something heavy. An old filing cabinet is hard to budge but I nudge it towards the door. It's plodding progress and as I work I can hear the banging build. I hear wood splinter and oak crack as the lock fixings are ripped from their home. They're in.

I hear a succession of footsteps grow louder on the bare wooden stairs. I just manage to push the cabinet up against the packing cases as the banging starts again. This time, there is only an inch and a half of beech between me and the marauding mob of bald-headed men. I panic. There's nothing left I can use to block their passage. The cabinet quivers from their battering. And then voices.

We know you're in there. Why don't you just give yourself up? It'll be easier for you in the long run.

You can either open the door or we'll break the door down.

It's your door.

It's your choice, mate.

I say nothing.

The banging builds and the shouting rises. I can feel it pounding in my brain. I retreat into a corner. I curl up into a ball and put my hands over my ears, my eyes shut tight. The noise swarms around my head. Its vibrations swoon and gibber. I don't know how long this goes on for, but suddenly I'm aware of silence. I relax my muscles, remove my hands from my ears, and slowly open my eyes. There in front of me, a mere six feet away, is the tall bald-headed man. I flinch.

Are you okay? he says.

I stare with incomprehension. He is no longer holding the crowfoot wrench. He looks puzzled, not angry.

I thought you were having some fit or something. I was gonna call my doctor. I've got her on speed dial on my phone, he says, before backing off and perching on some of the boxes, which are now spread in disarray across the room, where the entrance to my garret has been forced. My wife, she's epileptic see, he adds, by way of explanation.

I'm still trying to take all this in. I stare at the mess, at the magazines and books which only moments ago were carefully arranged. Where are the other bald men? I wonder.

What are you going to do with me? I eventually pluck up the courage to ask.

He laughs. Do with you? I just want to talk with you, mate. Listen, I'm here to help. He shrugs, as though his motives were never in doubt.

Then talk, I say, and then leave me in peace. You've done enough damage.

He gives me that puzzled look again, then he looks over to the door, hanging from its hinges, the screws barely clinging to rough splinters.

Oh, the doors, don't worry about that, mate. Kenny's a carpenter. He'll sort them out for you.

There's another long pause. I watch him rub his chin. Listen, I used to be like you, mate.

I shake my head in disbelief.

No, seriously, mate. I did. I had long, shiny chestnut hair, almost reached my shoulders, used to use special conditioner in it and everything.

So what happened?

I'm not sure whether to believe him but I want to. I want to believe there can be some good in these bald-headed men.

It's not worth it, mate, honestly. I've been there. You think you're being yourself, you think you're expressing your individuality, but what it is, see, it's selfish behaviour. To other people, see, it's like you're taking the piss.

I try and reason with him. But it's *my* hair, I can do what I want with it. Why can't I be free to choose?

He shakes his head wearily. Listen, fella, there's no such thing as freedom. Your freedom is at the expense of someone else's freedom, int it? I mean, how do you think it makes that lot feel out there? How do you think it makes *me* feel? You've got to think of the majority. You can't just think of yourself, see, it's hurtful.

But what about my feelings? I argue. What about what hurts me?

He rubs his chin again and shakes his head. There you go

again, see. It's all, me, me, me. You've got to realise there's something bigger than yourself. You're not the centre of the world, mate. If you disappeared tomorrow in a puff of smoke, what do you think would happen?

I shrug. I don't know, I say.

I'll tell you what will happen, fella. Fuck all is what will happen. You don't count. You don't register. You don't matter. Do you get it? He pauses, while he searches for another way of expressing it. Look, I don't mean to be cruel, it's not personal, right, but you're not important, none of us are. I'm not, that lot out there aren't, no one is, see. He rubs his chin again.

What's important is all of us. It's not the bloke who fixes your doors, or the bloke who pipes your water supply or the people who power your electricity. It's not the woman who brought you skriking into the world, it's not the woman who drives the bus taking you to work in the morning. It's not any one of us – it's *all* of us. If one ant dies, right, the whole colony doesn't fall apart, does it? It's stronger than that. Don't you get it? That one ant has no meaning without the rest of the ants. Do you see my point?

I feel so tired all of a sudden. My body is aching from my extended vigil. The sleepless nights, the constant running and ducking, watching my back. Walking in shadow, avoiding the multitude, my senses constantly heightened, my body awash with adrenalin. How easy it would be now to just give in, let go and submit my will to these people, to offer myself to them. I look over to the tall bald-headed man. He looks tired too. Tired of people like me, tired of these talks. How many of them has he had? I wonder. How many more like me has he had to convince? A strange feeling comes over me; it is one of empathy. I feel empathy for my persecutor, and it's as though he can sense it, for without another word spoken, he gently reaches into the inside pocket of his jacket and produces a bar of soap and a Bic razor.

It's a brisk, spring morning, and I'm standing at the bus stop waiting for the number 27. There's a mild chill to the breeze as it travels over my smooth pate and it makes my senses tingle, my skin prickle and then recoil ever so slightly. I feel alive, more alive than I have felt for a long time. Almost, you could say, reborn, for didn't I come into this world with my body naked and my head clothed? Now this time my head is naked, and my body clothed, for I am bald, just like the other men who stand at the bus stop, who offer me a kindly nod of acknowledgement, and I feel free in this world. Free to roam without torment, free to walk the earth without taunts and threats, free as every other bald-headed man walking on the skin of this spinning ball of sin and dust.

YOU ARE GOING BACK

You are going back to the place where you played as a child. It is a wood that was once an old rubbish heap and, as you enter along the same path you took twenty years ago, you see the bits of broken glass and rusting cans that always poked out from underneath the roots of the trees. The trees were planted too close together. A botched council job. Their trunks stretch up, gasping for the sun like a fledgling with its mouth gaping for a morsel of food.

Each tree has reached as high as it can, so that the trunks are gaunt and pallid and there are no branches until the very top. The whole place seems to totter. No birds come to the wood and nothing grows beneath the trees except damp mud-coloured mushrooms.

As you make your way along the path, you remember bringing a book on trees with you – you must have been eleven. You spent hours comparing leaf patterns and pictures of trees in the book, but the trees in this wood were beyond classification. They were deformed, the leaves drained of colour or too small to fit the illustrations. There is no one else here. Nor is there any evidence of anyone being here. That's what you liked about the place when you were a child. No one ever went there.

As you wend your way through the poles of bark, crushing the slimy fungus under foot, you remember finding a dead crow hanging by its legs. It was stiff and flies made a gauze of noise around it. It unnerved you, rather like Crusoe spotting the footprints. You thought you were alone, and you weren't. But there was never any other sign of life and you soon forgot about that dead bird. As you wander, the familiar smell fills your nostrils. It's a stale, fusty stench. Not too unpleasant once you get used to it.

You were twelve the last time you visited this place. That's when your mum left your dad. It was funny, inside you always knew that one day they would part, and yet it came as a shock. You were watching Tom and Jerry. Your mum and dad were in the kitchen. You hadn't noticed them talking. But then you noticed the silence.

Philip?

Your mum's voice. Even this is an omen. They call you Phil most times, except when there is something important to say, or when you are in trouble.

Yeah?

They have something they would like to discuss.

You switch off the television, the fizz of black screen in some way significant, and you walk slowly into the kitchen. Your mum looks at your dad, as though to prompt him. He looks back, wounded, and then turns to you.

What it is, Phil … me and your mum…

He tells you it's not easy. He tells you that when you're older you will understand – but he isn't saying anything. His voice peters out. He looks at his wife again and then back at you. He puts his hands to his eyes, as though he's ashamed to look at you. Your mum seems to view the man before her with disgust.

It's your mum who speaks. She tells you they're splitting up. She tells you it's for the best. She tells you your dad is moving out.

You don't know why, but you can't stop it. Hot tears roll down your cheeks. Why are your parents doing this? Your mum is lovely and your dad is a laugh. Of course they argue, but you remember the good times. The holidays, the day trips, snuggling up together on the sofa on wet Saturday afternoons to watch a *Carry On* film, your mum coming in with a fresh pot of tea and warm buttered toast.

Don't cry. It's no one's fault. It's just sometimes grownups can't live together. It doesn't work, even though they want it to work.

Why has your mum said this? Why has she used the word 'fault'? For some reason now, you're thinking it is someone's fault, and you're thinking it's your fault. *You* made them split up. So many times the arguments your parents had were because of you. Because your mum had been too strict and your dad had told her she was crushing you. You'd listened at the door. Or other times your mum had blamed your dad for being too soft on you. For not supporting her. So it was your fault for being bad.

There used to be a pond in the middle of the wood where the trees thinned out. You walk to that clearing. You want to know if it's still there. For some reason you can't put into words, it's important. Will it still be there after all this time? You've heard of a Koi carp that lived for over two hundred years, so maybe it will be. It was the last thing you did before you moved out with your mum. The house was for sale. Your dad's Koi carp collection had to go. Your dad was moving to a flat in town. There was no room for the fish there. There was a man coming to buy the fish off your dad. Twenty fish in all. You don't remember a time before the fish arrived.

You don't know why you did it, but that night, you crept into the garden with a plastic bag. You took the net by the side of the pool, the pool you helped your dad first dig out, then build, then line, then fill. The old pool had become too small. The fish had grown. You scooped out the smallest fish from the water and put it in the bag with some water from the pool. You called this fish Bruno – you don't remember why. You carried the bag all the way to the wood, to the clearing in the middle, to the pond.

Now you're a man with your own son. Your son is only five years old. How can he understand what you didn't understand at twelve? It was the one thing you promised yourself you would never do. You would stick it out, for the sake of your son. But things have got so bad between you and your wife, that in the end you have to accept that it's better for Josh, your son, if you do split up.

Your wife is right, what sort of house is Josh living in? One of constant arguing or one of ominous silence. You still love your wife, but there are too many differences. The differences that brought you both together. She is outgoing, and you liked that. It made it so much easier at parties. You were no longer the one who stood in the corner looking at the record collection or the one taking books off the shelf, pretending to read them. With your wife nearby you felt more confident. You were able to talk easily with people you'd never met before. But she wanted to go out all the time. She called you boring for wanting to stay in.

Perhaps you are, but your job means long hours and you're too tired in the evening. Besides, it always meant getting a baby sitter, and to you it just didn't seem worth it.

The trees are thinning out, giving the forest floor light enough to grow ferns. The path has run out, and you pick up a branch, to bushwhack your way through. It isn't much further as you remember. You agreed that it's better for Josh if there is one home where he is based. Your new place is a one-bedroom apartment, not really suitable for a five-year-old. You also have to be out first thing, to get to work. You agreed to look after Josh at the weekends. But it doesn't seem fair. You want to spend equal time with your son. Why can't he spend one week at your place and one week at his mum's? Or three-and-a-half days a week with you and three-and-a-half days a week with her? Don't be ridiculous, she said, he won't know whether he's coming or going.

At last you reach the middle of the wood. And there it is, the clearing and the pond. As you walk towards it, you can smell a vile, almost septic stench emanating from the water. As you come closer you can see a green scum on the surface. There are greasy green leaves. They form a shiny skin. You take the stick you've been using to clear a path and use it to sift the scum. The movement of the dank rotting foliage fills you with disgust.

The water is black and brackish. It looks like stale coffee. The stench is nauseating. You stare into the treacly sump, mesmerised by its stagnant inertia. It's a mirror that reflects only the hollow at the centre of your pupils. It's a mirror that throws up only shadows. You see a glutinous bubble rise to the surface and burst. Is this a sign of life in the murk? Surely nothing could live in this putrefaction.

But there it is, rising to the surface, a thick-skinned fish. Its scales grey and frayed. Its gaping mouth, slimy and emaciated. Its hard, glassy eyes, like a shark's. It stares into you. It has aged and altered, but you recognise it – Bruno. Does it remember you? You feel a shudder travel down your spine. You look at each other. What must it think of this mud that was once a pond?

You stand up and then you're running. Running through the narrow gaps between the trees. Dry dead branches snap under your feet. Mushrooms collapse; the flesh rips, the stalks crush.

When you get to your car you're panting. You are wet with sweat. Why did you run away? What came over you? You will get a bag, like you did twenty years ago. You will get a bag and return, and you will find a home for that fish. That's what you will do.

As you drive back to your apartment, you wonder where you'll put the fish. There's no room. You still have boxes of stuff to unload. There's no way she will take it. Apart from anything else, her new boyfriend would reject the idea on principle. You don't get on with him, for obvious reasons, but you feel that her new boyfriend is deliberately making it hard for you.

Last Saturday you called to pick up Josh. You were taking him for a pizza, and then to the cinema, but her boyfriend had taken him out shopping for some football boots. He never showed any interest in football when he was with you. She said she was sorry, he'd be back soon. But she didn't invite you in. She made you sit in your car for over two hours, until he returned. It turned out Josh had already seen the film. Her new boyfriend had taken him.

Back at your place, you put the kettle on. You're not thirsty but it's a comfort. You sip your tea from the mug she bought you when you first started seeing each other. You sit surrounded by unpacked boxes. The fish seems a long way from where you are now. You hold the mug, remembering the day you took it from its wrapping. You stare at it for a long time. Eventually, you hold the mug to your cheek to feel its warmth. The drawing on the mug made you smile once. It's a picture of a dog on top of its kennel. It reads: all is not lost.

THIS IS WHERE YOU GET OFF

She had her bags packed, but where was she going? She tried
not to think about it. There weren't many people on the bus.
It was after rush hour. Just the usual mums going to play-
group, lads going to sign on and old people going to Morrisons. She thought about the note she had left him. Where
had that come from?

> *Tom, it's over. I'm sorry. We've tried to make it*
> *work – but there's nothing left to try now. Just this*
> *spent, dead feeling. What has kept us together is*
> *quite simply habit. I hope you understand.*
>   *I do love you,*
>   *Claire.*

That was the thing. She still loved him. And yet even when
they'd met, in that dizzy rush of feeling, even then she knew
that at some point it would come to an end. She stared at
an old couple sitting opposite each other. They looked at
each other without seeing. He was wearing a mac and a flat
cap. She was wearing an anorak. It was like an exhibit in a
museum or even an art installation. Not a grain of life left
in them. Two husks. Dry and empty and lifeless. It was too
late for them but it wasn't too late for her. It wasn't too late
for Tom.

She was distracted from her thoughts by a small boy. He
was three, perhaps four. He was clinging to the handrail,
staring at her. She stared back without realising what she
was doing. Then the boy pulled a face. It made her smile.
She pulled a face back and the boy responded with an even

more exaggerated expression. It made her laugh. She looked around to see if anyone had noticed, but no one had.

Claire thought about her sister. Claire was heading into town. It would be easy to catch another bus to the other side of the city where her sister lived. She had a spare room. Claire could stay there until she got herself a flat. One of the new apartments near the river. She wouldn't mind, would she? They had not got on at all when they were kids, but they seemed to now. They weren't mates, too much history, but there was a family bond. Surely that counted for something. That's why family was so important. Your friends, even your lovers, they didn't have those roots. In the end, you could always go back to your family.

Now her mother and father were both dead, her sister was the only family she had. Surely she wouldn't turn her away? The small boy was standing up. He was running up and down the aisle, bumping into seats, making it a game. He was playing pinball, with himself as the ball. He made exaggerated bumping noises each time he banged into something. She looked around to see how the other passengers were reacting. The old couple hadn't even noticed. The two lads were staring out of the window. And the two mums with prams at the front of the bus were chatting to each other. He had the right idea. Treat it like a game. That's what life was, just a game, and if you took it too seriously you forgot it was a game.

What about her friend Jess? She had a spare room. It wasn't much, but it would do for a few days. Perhaps she should ring her first, but she had no credit on her phone. Would she be in now? No, she'd be at work. She'd meant to keep in touch with her but when she'd started going out with Tom they'd sort of drifted. They were still close when they talked on the phone, and they would often poke each other on Facebook, but somehow they never seemed to find time to actually *be* together.

Gone were the days of going out and getting drunk, flirting with some lads in a bar; later, a bit of raunchy dancing in the club, then back to Jess's to chill, a coffee and a giggle as they dissected the evening. Were those days gone forever? Jess was so career-minded now. Those days seemed encapsulated in a clear impenetrable bubble, so close and yet unreachable.

The old man was fidgeting in his pocket. He took out a bag of boiled sweets. He took one from its wrapper and popped it in his mouth, seemingly without thinking. He put the packet back in his pocket. He didn't offer his wife one. Perhaps he knew she didn't like them. Or perhaps he'd just forgotten to ask. Perhaps the whole sequence of actions was carried out without any thought at all. The small boy was close to them now. He was climbing over the seats, wriggling like a maggot or a snake. He seemed to be enjoying himself. Had the old couple even noticed? They seemed to stare out at nothing.

She felt envious of the small boy. Part of her wanted to join in. To be a snake, to be a maggot. To climb over the seats, just for the fun of it. But she was too self-conscious. And in any case, how would people react? They'd think she was mad. They'd probably call the police or a doctor, get her sectioned under the mental health act. Lock her away in some asylum.

At what age? she wondered. At what age does it stop being acceptable to pretend to be a snake on a bus? Eight or nine probably. This is what they gave you if you were lucky, eight or nine years and then you'd better start acting sensible. By that age, hormones were already starting the slow mutation into adulthood.

She looked to the rest of the passengers. The mums were still chatting. The lads still staring out of the window. No one else was taking any notice. By now the boy had worked his way up to the seat in front of her. She smiled at him. He stared back, looking straight into her, then *he* smiled, with his mouth and with his eyes. It made her feel warm inside. Like his hands were touching her.

Hello, she said.

At first he didn't react. But then he smiled again.

23

Having fun?

He nodded his head. It was funny, but he didn't appear to be with anyone. She looked around again. The old couple, the two lads and the two mums. None of them seemed to acknowledge him. The most likely candidates were the mums. But they hadn't looked up once. Occasionally they had looked in their prams, but they hadn't looked at the boy at all. She wondered if the parents were upstairs. She supposed they must be, but why would they let their boy play downstairs on his own? It wasn't safe. Whoever they were, they didn't deserve him.

He was still staring at her.

Where's your mummy? Where's your daddy? He didn't seem to understand her question. Perhaps he spoke a different language.

Are they up there? She pointed to the stairs. The boy shook his head. She tried again.

Where's your mummy and daddy?

Not got none.

You've not got a mummy?

He shook his head.

Or a daddy?

He shook his head.

But who are you with? The boy shrugged his shoulders.

Are they upstairs? Again the boy shook his head.

He must be with someone. The bus driver wouldn't allow a boy of that age to get on the bus on his own. She tried again.

Where do you live?

The boy seemed surprised by her question. Perhaps he hadn't heard her properly.

Whereabouts do you live?

Live here.

Yes, but whereabouts?

Again, the boy seemed not to understand her question.

On the bus.

You live on the bus?

He nodded his head. He mustn't understand her question, she decided. She turned to the old couple.

Excuse me, is this boy with you? They looked at her blankly. She got up and went to the two lads.

Excuse me, is this boy with you? They both shrugged and carried on looking out of the window. She walked further down the bus. She approached the mums.

Sorry, can I just ask, I'm trying to find out who this boy is with. You don't happen to know, do you? One of the girls raised her eyebrows to the other one and gave her a look, as if to say, who is this nutter? Claire went bright red. She went up the stairs, but when she got to the top deck there was no one there.

When she came back downstairs the bus was stopping. It was her stop. This is where she would have to get off if she was to catch another bus out of town. She grabbed her bags from the rack at the front and jumped off. The bus pulled away. As it did, she noticed the small boy. He was sitting on the back seat now and he was waving at her. She watched as he waved and waved until he disappeared. How strange. Nobody had seemed concerned about the boy at all. She couldn't leave it like this. She'd have to do something. She tried to push the thought out of her mind. There was nothing she could do. The bus had gone now. She picked up her bags and made her way to the station.

The air was damp and above her the clouds were heavy, but it wasn't going to rain, it would just stay like this all day. She was at the station now and she was looking at the time-tables. But still she hadn't decided whether to go to Jess's or her sister's. Well, she couldn't go to Jess's. Jess would definitely be at work. Her sister's it was, then. There was a bus in fifteen minutes. She'd get a coffee while she waited.

As she sipped from the Styrofoam cup the image of the boy loomed into view. How could she leave him like that on a bus, alone and defenceless? She went to the information office.

Excuse me, I'd like to report an incident.

The uniformed man looked up.

I see.

The bus I've just got off. The number 606.

What about it?

There was this boy on the bus. Only, he didn't appear to be with anyone.

Would you like a complaint form?

No, it's not a complaint. I'm worried. About the boy. I'd like you to make some enquiries.

The uniformed man seemed to view her with distaste.

You'd like me to make some enquiries, would you?

Yes, if you don't mind.

And what enquiries would they be, then?

Well, doesn't the bus have a radio? Can't you contact the driver?

The man was ignoring her now, shuffling some papers. She could feel herself getting annoyed.

Look, there was a boy on the bus and he was on his own. He was only three or four years old. Don't you see?

The man paused for a moment. He hated these awkward customers. Why couldn't she just ask for a timetable, or a complaint form like the rest of them?

Okay. Right. A 606, you say?

Yes, that's right. Heading towards Holmewood estate.

Hang on a minute then.

The uniformed man stood up and disappeared through a door at the back of the office. A queue of impatient people had formed behind her. The man at the front of the queue gave a tut. The rest of the queue shuffled. Some shook their heads, as though she were a troublemaker. One of the men turned to the woman standing next to him.

There's always one, isn't there? he said under his breath.

The woman nodded.

The uniformed man re-appeared. Right, I've had a word.

What did he say?

It seems you're right. There is a boy on the bus. And he appears to be unaccompanied.

What did I tell you?

Yes, well, there you go. Are you happy now?

What on earth could he mean?

Happy? What's it got to do with happy? I want you to do something about it.

Do something? Like what?

Stop the bus. Take the child to the police. I don't know, something.

You don't appear to know what you want.

Look, we need to do something. Surely.

Now listen here, if the boy was causing some trouble then yes, we could report him, but according to the driver he's sat at the back minding his own business. I can hardly report someone for minding their own business now, can I?

But he's only three or four years old. He's just a child.

Child or no child, if he's conducting himself in a civilised fashion, there's nothing I can do, I'm afraid.

Claire was exasperated. She took her bags and her coffee and sat back down. She sat there for over an hour, not knowing what to do. Should she go to the police? Yes, that was the best thing. She traipsed with her bags across town to the police station. But to her surprise, the policeman on duty had exactly the same reaction.

I'm getting nowhere here. Isn't there another policeman on duty I can speak to?

Another policeman?

Yes, is there someone in charge?

He seemed to find this amusing. Oh, deary me. That's a good one. Now do me a favour, stop wasting police time. There's all sorts out there, you know. Don't you think we've got enough to be getting on with?

She took her bags again and walked out. She walked on but she was tired. She found a bench beneath a tree and sat down. She watched the people rushing about from place to place, joyless and unfeeling. At least that's what they seemed to her. At last she decided to go to the depot. She'd find the driver and have it out with him.

Claire was hot and panting when she got there. She'd underestimated how long it would take her. The road out of town to the depot was steep and a lot longer than she had remembered. She walked around the bay where the buses were parked up. There was the 606 in a vacant space, its lights off and its doors locked. She trudged across to the drivers' rest room. She opened the door marked 'private' and looked around. The drivers, all men, all in uniform, looked towards her. They stared at her as if they were working out what she was. Then they went back to what they were doing: reading the paper, eating a sandwich or playing cards.

Then she spotted him. Her driver. She approached him. He was eating a bacon sandwich with his hat on his knee. He had bits of red sauce in the corners of his mouth.

Excuse me, were you driving the 606 this morning?

That's right, love. He spoke with half-chewed bacon and bread in his mouth.

Did you see a boy on the bus? About three or four years old?

Oh, it's you, is it? Listen love, I'm on my break, so if you don't mind –

Actually, I do mind. I'm not going to put up with it.

I see. He swallowed the chewed food and took a sip from his mug of tea.

And what the Nelly do you want me to do about it then?

Well, I mean, aren't you going to report it? I mean, did you take him to the police station?

The driver laughed. He put his hand up to his mouth to stop himself spraying bits of sandwich.

Now why would I be going doing that?

Well, I mean, aren't you concerned? A boy of that age on a bus on his own?

Listen, love, the boy is perfectly capable of looking after himself.

So you admit it then?

Admit what?

Admit there was a boy on the bus.

Course there was. That's where he lives.

I, I beg your pardon.

Look, love. That boy, he lives on the bus. Been there as long as I can remember.

He took another bite of his sandwich.

He's perfectly happy, so stop all this bloody mither and let people get on with their business. Now if you don't mind –

But, but, I don't understand. How can he live there? What does he eat? Where does he sleep?

The driver put the sandwich down. It was clear he wasn't going to get a decent run at it until he'd got rid of this woman.

Look, I'm just the driver. Don't expect me to have all the answers. Listen, I'll tell you what. Come with me. I'll show you something.

He led her to a back room full of monitors. Some of them were playing live feedback from the CCTV cameras positioned in the station and on the buses. The driver went to a central computer and started clicking a mouse.

All our buses are wired up and it's fed back here. It's recorded on a big server. Two years' worth of stuff on there. Have a look at this. This is from last year.

He pointed to a monitor which was playing footage from the 606 bus. She watched. Nothing seemed to happen. There were a few people sitting down. Motionless. Then she noticed it. There was the small boy crawling over the furniture like she had seen him do.

There you go. Now if we go back to the earliest records…

He started clicking the mouse again. Here we are. Two years ago.

She watched the monitor again. For a minute or more there was nothing. The bus stopped. Some people got off, some people got on. They sat down and the bus started moving again. Then she saw it. The small boy. He was running up and down the aisle as though he were a pinball, just as she had observed him that morning.

The driver switched the monitor off. Satisfied now?

She didn't know what to say to him. She took up her bags and left the room.

When she got home that evening, Tom was in the kitchen preparing a meal. He spoke without looking at her.

Wine's on the table.

She sat down at the table. Her feet felt heavy and her body was tired. She took the bottle and pulled out the cork. She poured some wine into both glasses. She took her own and drank gratefully from it. It tasted good. She could smell the food, garlic and onions frying together.

It won't be a minute. I've made that pasta sauce you like.

He stirred the pan with a wooden spoon. She noticed the note she had left. It was still there next to the kettle. It was hard to tell whether he'd read it or not. He took out two plates from the cupboard above the cooker. He poured out the pasta, then the sauce. He garnished it with some fresh basil and some grated parmesan. He switched off the hob and brought the plates over. He plonked hers on her mat and sat down opposite.

So then, he said as he picked up his glass. What sort of a day have you had?

MAKING CONTACT

She found him sleeping in the barn again, with the dogs. He was naked. There were spots of light on his body from the holes in the roof and the walls. The three dogs were curled up around him. She shook him awake. He seemed surprised to see her. He had no recollection of how he'd got there. She went back over the day with him, his routine: breakfast, shower, taking Emily in her pram through the park ... but the rest was a dark hole. The last thing he remembered was walking from the bus stop.

Where had he been? He didn't have a headache and he didn't feel hung-over in the least. She helped him up and he brushed the straw from his skin. They walked into the kitchen and she made them both a cup of tea. They sat at the table.

What on earth...

She didn't finish the sentence. She looked at him; at his feet full of mud, the straw still stuck to his knees and lodged in his hair. She looked him in the eyes and still she said nothing.

What happened to you? she asked, eventually. You must have some idea.

He wasn't looking at her but at the wall behind her, at its magnolia paintwork. I don't know, he said. I've no idea.

She put the mug down on the table and put her head in her hands. She wanted to laugh but instead she sighed. Where have you been, Paul? Where are your clothes?

He was still staring at the wall. She saw he was staring at a bubble where damp had lifted the paint from the plaster. She thought, quite calmly, I'll have to get the sandpaper and paint pot. I'll have to find the brush and the scraper.

I don't remember what happened, he said at last.

She finished the dregs of her tea and took her empty mug over to the sink. She placed it in the bowl of soapy water. She looked at the clock.

Okay then, what's the last thing you remember?

I was walking down the road. I was walking from the bus stop.

Were you walking home?

He had to think about this because he always got off the bus and walked home, but now she asked that question he remembered something else.

No, that's the funny thing, now I think about it. I wasn't walking home.

So where were you going?

I don't know.

What direction?

I was walking towards… His mind was blank but then the image popped into his head like a photograph. I was walking towards a field.

A field?

Yes.

What sort of field?

Just a field. A farmer's field, I think. Full of wheat.

And did you get to this field? Did you go into the field?

I don't know.

Karin sighed again and shook her head. Well you must have been drinking, she said at last. Like last time.

But that was the thing, he hadn't been drinking. He would know if he'd been drinking. He would feel it on his tongue, that dryness. He would feel remnants of the spirits on the roof of his mouth and around his gums. He would feel it in his head, that dull ache or that pounding thud. He would even feel it in his eyes.

I don't think so, he said.

This is ridiculous. I've got to go to work. I won't put up with this, Paul. You must remember something.

He just stared at the wall and shook his head. She reached for her coat and bag. She went to the door.

I've got to go to work. I'm late, she said. We'll talk about this later. Emily's sleeping. She'll need a bottle when she wakes up. Karin closed the door behind her.

They talked later that evening when she came home from work, but Paul couldn't tell her much. She became increasingly angry, accusing him in the end of having an affair. They'd agreed twelve months ago, when she found out she was pregnant, that he would give up his job at the call centre and she would go back to work six weeks after the baby was born. As a nurse manager she was on more money than him. It was a financial decision they had both agreed on. But it had caused Paul to act strangely. Some nights he was silent. Other nights he would go to the pubs in the village on his own and return drunk. On two separate occasions, he had woken up in the barn with the dogs because he'd forgotten his keys and had returned late and had not wanted to wake her. But he had always been fully clothed and he had always remembered what had happened.

Come on, think, Paul. I won't put up with this. You better come up with a good excuse or I've had it with you, Paul, I really have.

They were sitting in the living room. The television was on mute. There was a scene from a soap on the screen. A couple arguing. Paul could see the woman's mouth opening wide as she shouted at her partner. Then the camera cut to the man's reaction. He was red with rage and pacing the room. He was also shouting. Perhaps Paul should shout, perhaps Paul should get angry. After all, he was the one being accused of doing something he hadn't done. He was innocent.

I know one thing, he said at last.

This better be good, she said.

This ... this place... He indicated his surroundings with the wave of his arm. It's not my home.

What are you talking about?

Karin stood up. They'd argued before about her taste in cushions. Was that what this was about, a protest over soft furnishings? She wanted to hit him, but she didn't. She crossed the room. I'm going to bed, she said, and she slammed the door behind her. It was only eight o'clock.

The next night when she returned home she confronted him again. He was sitting in one of the armchairs staring at a blank television screen. He didn't even look up when she came in. She asked after Emily. She was upstairs sleeping, he said, still staring at the black square of glass. She threw her bag onto the sofa. The plates and mugs from breakfast were still on the table. He hadn't even bothered to remove the empty beer tins which he must have been drinking after she went to bed.

Snap out of it, Paul. I won't put up with this, she said. You said you were fine about me working. You said you were happy to give up work.

It's nothing to do with that. It's nothing to do with you.

Really? Is that right? Well, what is it to do with then?

He said nothing for a long time. She sat down on the sofa next to where she'd thrown her bag and she stared at him. She wanted answers. He looked away from the black screen for the first time and made eye contact.

It's me, he said. Something has happened.

What are you talking about, Paul? What's this all about?

I've remembered, is all he said.

Remembered what? Go on then, what have you remembered?

I've remembered what happened.

So tell me.

You won't believe me, Karin. There's no point.

Try me, Paul, just tell me! She was shouting again now.

I … I met some…

He stopped talking and struggled to form the words.

So I was right, she said. You've been seeing someone else.

It's not like that, he said. I've only seen them once.

Them? How many are you seeing?

It's difficult to say. There were a number of them. I couldn't tell you how many.

Paul, what the hell are you going on about?

In the field. There were a number of them. And they spoke to me.

Did they? They spoke to you. Who spoke to you, Paul? What are you talking about?

I'm one of them, Karin. I'm not… He hesitated, aware of how what he was about to say would sound, but he was filled with conviction. It was the truth. I'm not from this place.

Paul, you better start talking sense or –

They said they'd come back for me, Karin. To take me to where I'm really from.

Wha! What?

She stood up. She couldn't take this. Was he having some sort of nervous breakdown? Was it a psychotic episode? She was in general nursing, not psychiatric nursing, but she had friends who worked in the field.

I think you need help, Paul. I'm going to make a phone call.

A few days later they both went to see a psychiatrist Karin's friend had recommended. Paul didn't want to go, but Karin insisted. They sat in the psychiatrist's room and Karin explained everything. The psychiatrist listened to what she said and then turned to Paul for his side of the story. Paul merely reiterated what he had already told Karin. The psychiatrist asked to speak to Karin separately. He said there wasn't much he could do. He appreciated the strangeness of it all, but Paul was neither a danger to himself nor to others. He couldn't section him. Karin explained that she didn't want him sectioned. She just wanted him back. The way he had been before.

The psychiatrist suggested Paul come in to the hospital for a week so that he could monitor him. But Paul refused. Without Paul's consent there was no way forward. He suggested Karin keep an eye on him. He suggested that she try and stay calm no matter how frustrating the situation was. And with that he had shrugged apologetically.

Karin tried to stay calm. Two weeks had gone by since that morning when he'd come into the kitchen naked, with mud on his feet and straw in his hair. She tried to pretend it had never happened. She went to work in the mornings and in the evenings she returned. They ate tea together and watched television. At weekends they walked together in the park with Emily in the pram. But they were not together. She could feel the force of it pushing them apart like opposing magnets. What could she do? Now she was at the kitchen table again, sitting opposite him, staring at him and wondering. Was he mad? Was it a way of drawing attention to himself? Did he feel left out now Emily had come along? But surely it should be *her* who felt left out. He was the one doing most of the caring. He was the one who spent his day with Emily.

The effort required to make the outside seem calm was starting to unseam her. She was not calm. She was confused and hurt. She felt rejected. She felt excluded. She was not part of this and had no way in. At work she could push it to one side, maintain a professional image. But as soon as she started driving home she could feel the panic rising in her stomach. He was not the man she had married. He'd changed and she couldn't find a way of getting things back to how they'd been.

Halfway home from the hospital she stopped the car. She had to do something, but what? She pulled into the retail park off the motorway and parked outside a bookshop. She went to the section marked Mind, Body and Spirit and started to scan the sub-categories: Fortune-telling, Feng Shui, Conspiracy Theories, Unexplained Phenomena. There it was, a whole shelf to itself: Extraterrestrial Beings. She flicked through some of the books. *The UFO Files: The Inside Story of Real-life Sightings, Roswell, The Mothman Prophecies*; then at last, *Alien Encounters: True Life Stories of Aliens, UFOs and Other Extra-terrestrial Phenomena.*

She sat down in one of the chairs provided and opened the book. The stories were all remarkably the same. Did the witnesses actually believe their stories or were they, as she suspected of Paul, attention seeking? Perhaps they had started off as lies but after time they'd become truths. It didn't matter. What mattered was her marriage to Paul. She could make herself believe him through an effort of will. A truth, in fact, was a lie, a lie that had come to pass, a lie that had hardened and become solid. Did it really matter that it had happened? If this was the only thing between them they could overcome it together as they had done with other obstacles they'd faced. She went to the front of the shop and paid for the book. She would drive home. She would take him out for a meal and she would tell him she believed him. It was that simple.

As she left the motorway and drove down the country lane which led to their village, Karin felt her spirits lift. Everything would return to the place it had been before. They would go on as normal and the mechanism of their life together would recalibrate – click back into place. But when she pulled up to the house, it was in darkness, and when she opened the door she found Emily on her own, crying. There was no sign of Paul.

There was a note on the kitchen table. The note was addressed to her. She read it through several times before placing it back on the table. How could he explain to Karin, or indeed anyone, what he'd seen. That he had seen a light like no other, a colour and brightness he could not describe. How he had felt someone or something touch him, in a way he'd never been touched before. How he'd heard the voices in his head, not through language, not through words, but direct meaning. It sounded mad, it felt mad even to recall it to himself now, but that was what it was. And he knew, he knew with a knowledge that was more than knowledge that they were coming back for him. And he knew when. The precise time and the precise location. And that was all it said.

She searched the house for signs of his leaving. He hadn't packed a bag or taken his toothbrush. She went to the kitchen drawer – he hadn't even taken his set of keys. She pulled out her phone and rang his number, but seconds later she heard his ringtone. His phone was behind the fruit bowl. He hadn't even taken it with him. He always took his phone everywhere he went. Everything was exactly where it should have been and everything was how it should be, with just one thing absent, and that was Paul. He couldn't have left. He wouldn't leave her and he wouldn't leave Emily. He must have just popped to the shop. But his wallet was in the kitchen drawer next to his keys. He would come back. She would make him come back. She would sit at the table and think hard until, like a magnet drawing iron filings around it, she would pull him into her zone.

THE NAKED MAN

The naked man was walking from the east to the west through a thick mist. He walked across scorched heathland and along a rabbit run which connected to a dirt track. A farmer must have set fire to the heather, he thought. They do that to keep the heather young. As he walked along the dirt track, his skin glistened from the moisture in the air. In the distance he saw the outline of two people approaching. They were a dark silhouette shrouded by a white fog.

As he continued, he saw that the two people were a man and a woman and that they were holding hands. The man had a map case round his neck. The naked man watched as the two people pointed to him and exchanged words. He could feel a knot of apprehension in his stomach. As they got closer, the naked man could see that the woman was embarrassed. The man with the map case approached the naked man.

Excuse me, I've read about you, and I just want you to know, I admire you greatly.

Thank you, said the naked man. He felt the knot slacken.

The three had stopped walking now and stood some distance apart.

You must get a lot of stick, said the woman.

Yes, I do, unfortunately.

It must be hard for you, said the man with the map case.

It can be, said the naked man. These two people had no idea how hard it could be.

The man with the map case pointed to the west.

You see that field over there?

Yes.

The path goes down the middle. It's a public right of way, but the field is owned by a farmer. He lives in that white barn on the hill.

The man with the map case pointed to a large detached farm building.

He's not a very nice bloke. You might want to avoid that field.

Thanks for your advice, said the naked man, but that's where I'm heading.

Well, if I were you, I'd avoid it, said the woman.

The naked man thanked the couple again and continued on his way. He often met opposition, and it was comforting to think that there were people out there who supported him. He'd been shouted at and laughed at. He'd had a sandwich thrown at him. He'd been pushed over by two men and kicked in the head. But he'd also had people join his cause. He'd been stopped one time by a man in a car, with a flask of soup and some cake. He'd told the naked man that he'd been looking for him and he wished him luck. There were other people who could see the truth, it wasn't just the naked man.

In no time at all, he reached the field the man with the map case had pointed to. It was surrounded by a dry stone wall about five feet high. There was a gap in the wall and a wooden gate. The naked man lifted the latch and entered the field. He made sure the gate was fastened again, before continuing to walk down the field. The field was steep and he could see that it went down to meet a river, and beyond that, a wood. Further still, clusters of houses indicated the edge of the town where he was heading.

There were three crows in the field, but as he approached them, they cried out and flew off, and he was on his own again. He had to walk quite slowly as the field became steeper. The grass was short and there were clumps of sheep excrement, but there were no other signs of the flock. They must be grazing in a different field, the naked man thought.

He was halfway down the field, when he saw a man approach from the south. He watched the man running and saw that he was carrying something in his hand. He was shouting at the naked man but he couldn't tell what he was saying. He felt the knot in his stomach tighten. He could carry on walking, but he decided to wait for the man, so that he could confront his own fear and hear what the man was trying to say to him.

As the man got closer, the naked man could see that he was carrying a hammer in one hand. He was wearing a waxed jacket.

You can't come through my field with no clothes on, the man with the hammer said.

Why not?

Look, it's my field, if I say you have to wear clothes, you have to wear clothes.

But this is a public right of way.

It's my field.

Well, it can't be your field, can it?

You what?

If this was entirely your field, you'd be able to deny access, but you can't, so therefore it's not entirely your field.

Listen, I've got kids. They can see you from the front window.

The man with the hammer pointed to the white barn on the hill.

What you're doing is disgusting.

What's disgusting about the human body?

My daughter's only six.

And when she was born, was she wearing any clothes?

I don't think that's any of your business.

All I'm saying is that we are all born naked. It's our natural state. Why does that disgust you?

I don't have to explain myself to you, mate. I don't want my girl getting upset.

I think the best thing you can do is to leave me alone, while

I walk through your field, along this public footpath, which I'm entitled to do. I mean no harm to you or your family. I'll be gone in two minutes, and you'll never need to look on my offensive nakedness again.

I can't do that.

Why not?

If you don't put some clothes on, I'll ring the police.

I don't have any clothes.

The naked man held his hands up. He was completely naked and had no bag with him. It seemed evident to him that he had no clothes. He carried on walking. The man with the hammer shouted to him.

I've warned you! I mean it!

Then the man with the hammer ran up the hill, towards the white barn.

The naked man could not understand people like the man with the hammer. He could feel anger heating inside but also knew, after many years of practice, how to control that anger. What had the hammer been for, in any case? Perhaps he was fixing a fence, but still, didn't he know how intimidating it was to confront someone while clutching a hammer?

As he reached the river, the naked man could see that it was pure and clear. There were two streams that met to form a strong flowing beck, which opened out to create a deep pool of clean, fresh water. There were foxgloves and thistles along the bank. Purple bells and purple pompoms. There were bees and hoverflies and lots of butterflies: cabbage whites, small tortoiseshells, meadow browns. He watched them flit from flower to flower. There were fish rising to the surface of the water, catching the insects that skated over the top. He wondered what sort of fish they were.

He looked up to the sky. The mist had lifted. There were thin florets of clouds around the sun, so that fine lines of sunlight filtered through to form a cathedral of white shafts. He lay back on the grass and could feel the soft, cool earth beneath him. He wished there were words to describe this feeling, this sense of completeness, this sense of nowness. He watched the light and he listened to the birds in the trees.

The naked man was hot. He'd been walking all day. He needed to cool down. He walked over to the pool of water and submerged himself into it. At first it was cold, and took his breath away, but as he swam, he soon warmed up and he felt energised by the water. He could stand up in it and feel the sandy floor of the beck under his feet. He dived under the water and felt the water wash through his hair. He came to the surface. The light sparkled and fractured as the ripples spread. He lay on his back and floated, looking up at the sun filtering through the clouds. It was this moment. This was what it meant. This was it: the truth.

He thought back to a sunny day when he was only five years old. He was walking with his mother and they had found a river that was deep enough to swim. His mother had wanted to swim in it, but she didn't have a costume. Then she'd said, what the hell. There was no one around, and they had stripped naked and swam together, enjoying the freedom of being one of God's creatures.

He climbed out of the water and lay on the bank again. He could see rabbits in the distance and when he looked up to the sky this time, he saw, very high up, two buzzards in an upward gyre. Were they watching him, he wondered, or were they watching the rabbits? He could feel the heat of the sun on his skin as the water evaporated. He ran his fingers through his hair. It felt clean. He could close his eyes and go to sleep right now, merge with the landscape around him. But he had somewhere he was heading. It was important.

He stood up and had a look around. He saw a wooden bridge across the river and then a path that joined a bridleway. He would soon be clear of the country and on the edge of the town where he was born. He didn't remember the town. He'd been very young when they had moved away. But now he was walking home.

He crossed the bridge and walked up the bridleway, which

was steep at first but then levelled out. When he got to the edge of the town, he could see the housing estate where the path ran out. There was a road, and he could see that there were two cars parked along the road – police cars.

He experienced a feeling of unease, but then he reasoned that they were unlikely to be there for him – police cars were a feature of any modern town – and he carried on walking. As he drew closer to the road, he noticed a man standing close to the cars. He was talking to someone in the passenger side of the front car and pointing over in his direction. He was no longer carrying a hammer, but it was unmistakably the farmer the naked man had spoken to before who lived in the white barn.

He was just under a mile away from the house where he'd been born. He was hungry. He hadn't eaten since the day before. He tried to block the farmer out of his mind. He tried to block the police cars out of his mind, but as he got closer, he saw two uniformed men and one uniformed woman, get out of the car and join the farmer. They walked over to the path and formed a barrier.

As he approached them, he tried to clear his face of any expression.

Excuse me, could you make some room please? I need to get past, the naked man said.

One of the police officers replied, I'm sorry, but we can't let you go any further.

Why not?

We can't let you go any further, unless you cover your buttocks and genitalia.

I don't have any clothes.

The policewoman went back to the car and returned with a bag.

We've brought some with us, a tracksuit.

She opened the bag and took out a grey sweatshirt and jogging pants.

It's not an offence to be naked, said the naked man.

If you continue to refuse to cover your buttocks and genitalia, we will charge you with a breach of the peace, said a policeman.

And we can arrest you if we think there are reasonable grounds for believing a breach of the peace is taking place, said the other policeman.

There's a children's playground up the next street, said the policewoman.

A breach of the peace is defined as being an act done or threatened to be done which actually harms a person, or in his presence, his property, or is likely to cause such harm being done, said the naked man.

Correct, said a policeman.

I told you he could talk, didn't I? said the farmer.

How am I harming anyone? said the naked man.

Some people may be distressed by your appearance, said the policewoman.

Do you really think that? said the naked man.

I'm distressed, said the farmer. I find it very confrontational. It's a disregard for other members of the public, is what it is, particularly children. It's arrogant.

Please, Mr Gough, this is a police matter. Let us deal with this.

I'm just saying, his intention is to cause alarm.

The human body isn't offensive, said the naked man. You can't control what distresses people. Nakedness is not illegal. We are all born naked. If people are offended or upset by a naked man then that is their problem. Not mine.

See what I mean? said the farmer.

Please, Mr Gough, said the policewoman.

We'll give you one last chance, said a policeman. Either put these clothes on, or we'll have to arrest you.

But you can't prove I've harmed anyone.

We don't need to prove it. Not if there's a chance a member of the public will be harmed by your appearance.

Will you put them on? It will make things a lot simpler. We

don't want to arrest you if we don't have to, said the police-woman.

I can't agree to put the clothes on, said the naked man. If I agree to put the clothes on, then it means I think there is something wrong with being naked, which I don't. Don't you see? It's not possible for me to put them on.

Have it your way, said a policeman.

He told the naked man why he was being arrested, ex-plained his rights, then he took hold of the naked man, while the other policeman handcuffed him. They led him over to the first car and pushed him onto the back seat. There were a few other people gathered now. A man with a dog was shouting at the police car.

Oi! Leave him alone. You bunch of fascists.

The car pulled away and drove down the road. It turned left at the end and along the street the man was heading for. About halfway down he saw it: the house where he'd been born. He had no memory of his birth. He'd read about people that did, but he didn't believe them. His first memory was falling off his tricycle, aged three.

As he passed the house, he looked through the front win-dow, but he couldn't see anyone, just a black square. He sat back in his seat and thought, it was here that I was born, as naked as I am now. He was going to prison this time, he was sure of that – for a long stretch. But he knew that what he was doing was right. He held the truth in his mind. There was only the truth, that was all there was. He just had to keep hold of the truth, in all its nakedness.

MR JOLLY

I saw them through the window gorging themselves: starlings. I watched them harpooning the tender seeds, and was filled with a curious mixture of repulsion and recognition. Because when we watch birds, half the time we're thinking how like us they are, and the other half, how alien. And I wasn't sure which had repulsed me really, but watching them feast, it made me think how reptilian starlings are. Something of the dinosaur in them. I went out and shooed them away, and I said to myself then, I've got to do something about them; but you know what, I didn't.

All over summer I thought about it. Now it's October and my usual rich harvest has amounted to a meagre handful of kale, carrots, parsnips and a few spuds. How's that going to sustain me over winter? I put the root vegetables in boxes in the cellar – they last longer that way. Then I took a large plank of wood and nailed it to a smaller plank of wood, so that I now held aloft a crucifix the size of a man. I had a sponge ball in the garden, about the size of a football. I think one of the local lads had kicked it over. It had been there ages, at least a couple of years, and the weather had got to it so that it was covered in a soft tuft of moss, where it had been exposed – a little thatch of fluffy hair.

I took it and skewered it onto the top of the crucifix. Then I went upstairs and got some of my old clothes. An old pair of jeans with a creosote stain on one knee. A jumper from Next that an aunty had got me for Christmas a few years ago. It was still in its wrapper. I was never going to wear it. First, it was navy. Navy's not my colour. Second, it was the wrong size. Third, it was wool and I've never been able to wear wool. Last of all, it was a jumper and I've never worn jumpers. I don't know what it is about them, I feel trapped by them I suppose. So, as a Christmas present it fell short of most of the criteria. Anyway, it suited my man better, so I put it on him.

I had a pair of gardening gloves that were past their best and I attached them to the end of his arms with some garden twine. I used masking tape to create a smile, and I burnt his eyes into the sponge ball with my soldering iron. Okay, it was never going to win a prize, but as soon as I looked at my work I felt a surge of ... what? Well, I've not been a parent, so I don't know, but I can only describe it as a fatherly pride.

His smile filled me with warmth. Such innocence, untarnished by the sins of the world. He stood there open-armed, smiling the smile of the guiltless. I hugged him. There was nothing for him to do, it's true, but I put him to work straight away. I fixed him right in the middle of the vegetable patch. Right there and then. His open arms seemed to be saying, look at all you behold, I will protect it from the scavengers and thieves of the world. I have taken all that you hold dear under the protection of my ample wings. Nothing can ever harm you now. And I went back inside, safe in the knowledge that from now on my autumn bounty would be plentiful. I was no longer alone.

Later that afternoon, I was making some cheese on toast and the funny thing was, there were two pieces. I'd made an extra piece. I ate it all myself, of course. My man, with his masking tape smile, was incapable of wantonness.

It was lovely having him there in the garden. I felt something lift inside me. I had been a bucket with a leak, and all the goodness had been seeping out. Only I hadn't noticed. And now I could see it and it lifted me. The hole inside me where my true self had been siphoned away was filled, and I felt buoyant again.

I even whistled a tune from childhood. We used to have to sing it in assembly. It hadn't stirred anything in me then but, whistling it to myself now, I felt a peculiar rush of emotion and, before I knew it, I was singing it at the top of my voice whilst marching round the room: *We plough the fields and scatter the good seed on the land…* As I sang, I swear, I saw my man curl his smile into a grin. A grin of contentment.

That night I dreamt I was in a forest. I was a boy again. There were horses running wild and bluebells everywhere. A small girl skipped, dressed in white with a chain of daisies. I was lying on the forest floor. It was rich and heavy with the musk of rotting vegetation. The girl kissed me on my cheek.

When she left, my cheek was tingling, and instead of a kiss there was a butterfly perched upon my now-young flesh. And as the butterfly took flight, a myriad of bells chimed from my belly … and at that point, I woke up. It was morning. A new day. I went to the window and I drew back the curtains. There he was – my man – yawning as the dawn broke. Dew festooned his skin like a jewel's glister. I knew then that everything would be okay.

That day we worked hard. I brought in some of the more tender perennials and mulched the borders with my own homemade compost. Also, I wanted to prepare the ground for the next spring. I dug up some of the turf and turned it over, encouraged by my man to be more productive.

It was a cool day but by lunchtime I was wet with sweat, and panting. I went inside and made us both a sandwich, washed down with a fresh pot of tea. It was then, as I rinsed the pot out in the sink, that I saw it. A magpie. It flew over my man and let its bowels open, evacuating its contents onto the top of his head. I ran out immediately, but what could I do? I was impotent. The bird's excreta was dribbling down his cheek.

I brought him in and sat him at the kitchen table. I filled a bowl with hot soapy water. I washed the stains from his face and gently patted him dry with a soft cloth. He smiled at me. There we go, I said, good as new. I made him some porridge. I sweetened it with honey. He seemed to enjoy the hot milky texture.

I sat down next to him with a cup of tea. I'm sorry, I said. I should never have left you on your own. As I sat there, in the silence, with just the gentle hum of the fridge, I had a feeling of completeness. I talked to him about my plans for the garden. I'd been thinking for a while about getting a greenhouse but it was a big expense. Not something to rush into. He sat there and listened.

Afterwards, I took the bowl and my mug over to the sink. I turned my back on him while I did the washing up. The pan was already sticking with the remnants of porridge. You have to wash it off straight away before the mixture sets. I scrubbed my mug, making sure I removed all the tannin stains. I stacked the pots in the drainer and stared out of the window. I looked at the patch where we had worked all morning. How wholesome it looked. The soil was so fresh. That's when I heard his voice for the first time. I could just eat a teacake, he said. I turned around. My man was smiling at me.

Did you say something?

He just smiled back. I thought I'd left the radio on at first. So I unplugged it and went back to the washing up.

I say, old chap, I could do with one of those marshmallow teacakes in that box.

There were indeed some marshmallow teacakes in a box, each one wrapped in red and silver foil. I took one and offered it to him, but of course, he didn't move to take it. His hands were fixed to the end of a plank. I took it out of its wrapper and let its circumference touch his masking tape mouth. I half expected it to open, but it didn't. Of course. So I opened my mouth and consumed the treat whole. I went back to the washing up.

Why have you made me?

I turned around again. He was smiling back benignly.

I'm sorry. Did you say something?

Yes. I questioned your intention. Why did you make me only to torment me?

His mouth had not moved, but I'd heard his voice distinctly. There was no mistake. It was as clear as a bell.

I didn't make you to torment you.

Then why flaunt your freedom? Why rub it in my face?

I made another pot of tea and sat back down at the table. I explained to him that I had made him out of love. He accused me of conceit. He accused me of sadism.

How so? I said.

Do you think it's fun, being me?

I asked him what I could do to make him more comfortable.

Take this bloody jumper off for starters. It's too tight around the shoulders. It's crushing me.

I pulled it over his head and placed it on the back of a vacant chair.

I'm bloody freezing now, he said. What do you think it is, old chap? Sort it out.

I went upstairs and opened my wardrobe. I had a green zipped fleece jacket that I'd hardly worn. I was saving it for winter. I took it off the hanger and brought it downstairs.

How's that? I said, zipping the front up to his neck.

Better. How about another teacake? There's a good chap.

We talked all afternoon. A right good natter. We spent most of the week chatting. Drinking tea. Eating porridge. We talked about so many things. For example, public transport. I made a point about buses. We both agreed that people who put their feet on the seating are unacceptable. On-the-spot fines, was my solution. My man thought this too lenient. He proposed a good flogging. On and on we chatted. We couldn't get enough of each other's company.

It was the start of November. The weather was on the turn. I'd brought everything in from the garden. The green leaves had turned golden and were falling from the trees.

There's a film on later, I said, washing my hands in the sink.

Which one? he said.

The Bargee. It's got Ronnie Corbett in it.

I've seen it before, he said. Lemon peel, what the bloody hell is that all about?

I thought you liked it, I said, drying my hands on a towel.

It's all right, I suppose.

You know, I do like these conversations, I said. We really set the world to rights, don't we?

You do, old chap. There's no shutting you up. Gets on your wick.

Are you beginning to … you know. I mean, you and me, we're good friends, aren't we?

You watch it if you like. I'm going to have forty winks.

I turned on the telly and settled down. There was a knock on the front door and I went to answer it.

Three boys, probably not even in their teens. They were collecting for their bonfire. I was eager to get back to my man and I sent them on their way. Only, when I went back to the kitchen, he was gone. I searched the house. I searched every room. I searched the garden. But still, there was no sign of him. I ran out of the house and up the street, after the boys, but there was no sign of them either. I came back inside. I didn't know what to do. That was two days ago.

And now I watch the flames from my upstairs window. The bonfire has been lit and on the top of the fire, there he is. But it's too late. There is nothing I can do except stare at the sickening spectacle and watch as my only friend in the world is destroyed before my eyes. As the flames reach the top of his fleece, the masking tape melts and his smile curls down. The boys cheer. I turn away. It is too much to bear.

Is life loss? Is this all there is? Each breath we exhale is a giving up, a death of life. I look around me, at the growing miasma. At the dust spreading like bacteria on every piece of furniture – the dust which is my flesh, leaving me, a shedding of myself, shrinking so that I will fit into my grave.

THE BUTTERFLY ON
THE CEILING

Watching Claire kneading the bread, you feel like you're intruding on something private. There are carrier bags full of groceries on the floor. You haven't seen Claire for a long time, but what people have told you is true. She's changed.

You don't mind me being here do you? you say.

Actually –

I was passing. It seemed rude not to.

I wasn't expecting you.

I was just going past your flat.

You weren't just going past her flat. It has taken you two bus journeys and a twenty minute walk. In heels.

I should've rung. I had some time to kill. And I just thought, it would be nice to say hello, seeing as you're only round the corner.

I see.

Does Claire believe you? It is hard to tell. She doesn't make eye contact and seems more interested in the dough than in you.

What's with all the bags? you ask.

Online shopping. It's just been delivered.

But, you've got a supermarket just up the –

It's easier, that's all.

It doesn't seem like Claire. Claire used to love going round the shops. It was one of the reasons she moved to Highgate. The delicatessens and specialist grocers. Fresh bread, fresh veg, fresh cheese, several good wine merchants.

Do you want me to help you put it away?

Claire doesn't look up, just shrugs. You look around the flat. Nothing much has changed from what you remember. You're looking for clues, but there is nothing out of place.

You've got it looking good, you say at last, feeling the need to say something.

It's just the same as before.

You've got a few new things.

I don't think so.

You feel awkward in Claire's presence and it isn't just the amount of time you've been away. Something in Claire is making you feel strange. You reach into your bag.

I brought us some wine.

I'm just in the middle of baking.

What is it you're baking anyway?

Bread.

Bread? Can't you just buy it from a shop like everyone else?

You mean it to sound amusing but there is irritation in your voice. Claire looks up for the first time.

I'm just making bread, Mary, okay. I didn't invite you here, and I don't see what it's got to do with you whether I'm baking bread or not.

Claire is staring at you and squeezing the dough with her fist. Try again, you think.

I think it's sweet that you're making bread.

You've done it once yourself when you were trying to sell a flat in Manor House. You'd read about it in a property magazine. The smell of baking bread is supposed to sell your place quicker. You take the bottle of red wine out of your bag and put it on the table next to Claire.

I've got two hours before my train.

Claire puts the loaf in the oven. She goes over to the sink and washes her hands.

Have a sit down.

She pulls out a chair for you, then takes a cloth and wipes the table. She places two glasses on the cleaned surface and roots for a corkscrew.

You okay with red?

You uncork the bottle and pour the wine into the glasses. You hand one to Claire.

I've just come back from Turkey.

You've been sailing Vic's boat. Claire sits down at the opposite end of the table.

Did you have a good time? she says.

Well, yeah. Only it was a bit windy. We didn't get to where we wanted to go. We started at Istanbul, went down the Aegean, stopped off at the Aegean islands. Stopped off at Naxos.

Where were you supposed to be going?

You explain that the plan was to sail south, under Greece and up the Adriatic, towards Croatia, but you ran in to a storm and had to change routes.

So you're okay then? you ask.

Fine.

You sure?

What's the matter with you? I've told you, I'm fine. I'm just baking some bread, that's all. I don't see what all the fuss is about. It's okay for you to sail around the world, twice, but I can't bake a loaf of bread, is that it?

I don't mean the bread. I don't mean the bread at all. But now you mention it, I do think the bread is a bit weird, yes… What sort of bread is it?

Look, it's just bread, that's all. An ordinary loaf of bread.

Who's it for?

What do you mean, who's it for?

You lean over and fill both glasses.

I was talking to Sarah, you say. You look at Claire to see her reaction but there isn't one. She came out to see me … on the boat.

Did she?

She said she'd seen you.

Did she?

On your birthday.

That's right. She came round here.

She said she'd tried to get you to have a party.

I didn't want to make a fuss.

She was worried about you.

Did she say that?

She did. Yes.

Well, there's no need, okay? I'm fine.

You sit back in your chair. It isn't very comfortable. You just want to talk to Claire, find out if the rumour is true, but this feels more like you're interrogating her.

She said you'd been acting … different.

What do you mean by that?

I didn't say it, *she* said it. You know what she's like. She can be a bit evasive. But she was worried about you and she said you'd been acting strangely.

Claire takes her glass and knocks it back in one.

And you were just passing? Just walking past? She gets up and goes over to the cupboard. She takes out another bottle of red and places it next to the empty one. It's a screw top. She opens it and fills both glasses. Sarah put you up to this.

I was just passing through.

The heat from the oven is starting to make the room oppressive. You stand up and take both glasses. You ask Claire to join you in the other room. You go through. You on the sofa, Claire in an armchair.

Look. She just thought it was a bit odd. I think it's a bit odd. About you keeping strange men in here.

What are you talking about?

She told me, Claire. She told me about the man.

There's nothing to it. I don't see what all the fuss is about.

Fucking hell, Claire. You invite a man you know nothing about to stay in your home. Apart from anything else, it's dangerous. You're on your own. You didn't know anything about him. He could have been anyone.

It wasn't like that.

Wasn't it?

You sit in silence for a while. Eventually Claire speaks.

It was late. It was raining. There'd been a storm. Someone was knocking on my door. I wouldn't normally answer it. But they were persistent. They kept knocking, and I thought, it being my birthday, I thought it would be someone I know. We'd been having this really humid weather. It had stormed a bit in the afternoon. For about an hour. Torrential rain. And it stormed again. Only much worse. You know I don't like lightning.

So what happened?

I answered the door… There was this man, stood there. He had long hair and it was dripping wet. He was shivering. He looked half-starved. He really did. He looked a wreck. He hadn't shaved, and he looked bedraggled. He had cuts on his skin. And… I don't know, he looked vulnerable, I suppose.

You let him in? You let a man you knew nothing about into the house?

I had to. What else could I have done?

You could have shut the door on him. You could've given him a number for a local hostel. You could've given him some money for a cup of tea and pointed him to the nearest café. You could've called the police, for fuck sake.

It was his eyes. He had such sad eyes. I knew a man with those eyes couldn't hurt anyone.

For fuck sake, Claire. Don't you realise how stupid you've been? Don't you realise what danger you put yourself in?

I'm fine. Nothing happened. I'm fine, okay?

But it could have. Don't you see? Anything could've happened. He could've raped you. He could've killed you.

But he didn't.

Why didn't you tell me?

Claire sloshes the wine in her glass. You take out a pouch of tobacco. You roll a cigarette.

Because I knew you'd have this reaction. I knew you'd get it all out of proportion. And I knew you'd judge him. I knew you'd judge me.

How else do you expect me to react? It was a crazy thing to do. It's just not like you.

Well, that's where you're wrong. That's where you are so wrong about me. Because that's exactly the way I am. I don't judge people. I don't automatically assume that every man is a rapist or a killer. And that doesn't make me naive, okay. That just makes me someone who doesn't judge someone, right?

You fiddle with your cigarette, not sure if you should ask if you can smoke it or not. There's a wall of formality between you that was never there before. Claire necks the remaining wine in her glass. She stands up.

Do you want some more? Claire says.

You empty your glass and pass it across. Go on then. I brought two bottles.

Thought you had a train to catch?

Claire passes you an ashtray.

You should've flown out to see me. You would've liked the Aegean.

Not really my style.

It used to be.

You and Claire went everywhere together at one point. Weekend trips, festivals, parties. But what was she doing now, holed up in her flat like a hermit?

When was the last time you went out?

This morning. I bought a paper.

No, I meant *out* out. As in a bar or a club. Somewhere where you get drunk, snog a dodgy bloke and end up being sick in your knickers.

It wasn't that long ago.

Yeah. Right.

You're relaxing now, the wine, your friendship is an ember warming through.

There's so much, out there –

So much what? you say.

Just … so much. In here it's simple. There are four walls.

There's a table. There's a sink. I can make bread… Out there. On the streets, in the pubs. In people's homes…

A woman was kidnapped the other day.

I heard about that.

She was walking through the park, and four lads in hooded tops, only about twelve or thirteen, kidnapped her. Kept her tied up in their den for days. They cut her fingers off.

I read about it in the paper. It was a one-off incident.

Was it?

'Course it was.

I feel like I don't know you. I feel like I've got to get to know you again… Tell me about this man?

Tell me about your sailing.

Well, we sailed. It was windy. There was a problem with the electrics. We didn't get to where we were going. That was it really. Vic's not that well. I don't know how long he can keep that boat going in his condition. That's why he's always asking me to sail it. He can't cope on his own.

Are you sure that's the only reason?

Oh, come off it. Vic! I don't think that's going to happen. I like them twenty years younger, not twenty years older. The third day in he caught me on deck with my tits out. That alone nearly gave him a heart attack. I did get off with a bloke though.

Who?

Wait till I tell you his name. I was drunk. He was Turkish. Kept calling me his 'sevgili'. He was a translator. And he was called Attila.

He wasn't.

Claire laughs. It's the first time you've made her laugh. You used to always be able to make her laugh and it makes you feel good to hear her chuckle.

He was. Attila the translator. I swear.

I don't believe you.

I swear. He looked good with his clothes on, but when he took them off –

59

What?

My God! He was so hairy. He had hair growing on his shoulders, all over his back –

Yuk!

He had the hairiest arse. It was like stroking a horse's mane.

Oh no. I couldn't.

It was too late then. In for a penny, in for a pound.

I'd have run away.

I couldn't. I didn't have any jeans on – or knickers for that matter.

You both laugh at that. The wine is creating a pleasant haze.

I'm sorry about what happened, you say.

What do you mean?

Between us.

Don't.

You're surprised by Claire's forcefulness. You sit in silence for a while, blowing out puffs of cigarette smoke, making the room fuggy.

So tell me about this man, you say.

I'd rather not.

Why not?

It's just. It's just private.

Oh, come off it. How can it be? I've told you about Attila the hairy-arsed translator, haven't I?

You wouldn't understand.

Try me.

It's nothing really.

Tell me what you thought, when he came to the door. You must've thought something. Weren't you scared? Weren't you at least a bit surprised?

That was the strange thing.

Go on.

Well, I think, under normal circumstances, I would, you know, have felt scared or something.

But you didn't?

No.

That's odd.

He was naked.

What?!

He didn't have any clothes on and his skin was glistening with rain.

He was naked? He had no clothes on? Why didn't you say that before?

It didn't seem important.

It didn't seem important! Are you having a laugh?

It just didn't.

Fucking hell, Claire. A naked man comes to your door with cuts on his skin. How bad were the cuts?

Nothing too serious. I washed them for him. I dressed them.

I don't believe this. A naked man comes to your door in the middle of a storm, in the middle of the night, with cuts on his skin and you bring him in and you dress his wounds. What on earth were you thinking of?

You weren't there. You don't understand. It wasn't like that.

So tell me more then.

If you'd seen him. I can't describe it really. But there was no hesitation. I didn't doubt him for a moment. As soon as I saw him, I felt, I don't know really, reassured by his company. There was just something incredibly tranquil about him. Like a still, clear lake.

Like a still clear lake?! Claire, get a grip. What are you talking about?

You weren't there.

So what did you do?

Well, he came in and I gave him some towels. I cleaned him up. He had a bath actually.

You let him use your bath?

He was dirty. So he had a bath. I made him some supper.

I don't believe this.

It was already made. I'd made some soup, and there was some left over. All I had to do was heat it up.

And did he eat it?

He did. He had two bowls of it. He said that my soup was perfect. He said that I was perfect.

Fucking hell, Claire! He was a nutter.

For a moment Claire seems shocked but then you both burst out laughing and everything is okay again.

So how did you get rid of him?

I didn't.

No way! He stayed?

Yes.

Where did he sleep?

You won't tell Sarah if I tell you, will you?

No, of course not. You didn't, did you? Did you?

No. Nothing like that. He slept in my bed.

Claire!

I slept on the sofa.

And nothing happened?

No. I promise. Nothing like that happened.

Well, here's me going all the way to Turkey for an adventure, and you get a naked man knocking on your door. I think you're both nutters. I do really. You deserve each other. You must have been drawn to each other.

You both laugh again.

He's gone though, right? you say.

Pardon?

The naked man? He's gone?

Of course.

You feel your stomach relax where you didn't even know you'd been tensing. You laugh again, out of relief.

Thank fuck for that. I thought for one minute then... Just for one minute... Oh well, it doesn't matter.

You finish off the second bottle. The timer on the oven rings.

Claire takes out the loaf and puts it on the bread board to cool. She walks back into the room with a third bottle. You take your shoes off. Your feet have been killing you for about an hour. Claire pours you both a glass of wine and watches you massage your feet.

Can I wash them?

What?

I'd like to wash your feet… Please.

Well…

Please.

I suppose.

Claire takes a bowl and fills it with water and some soap. She places it by the side of your feet. She takes your foot in her hands and lowers it into the water. You wince a little at the heat, but then feel the warmth and the water release the tension in your muscles.

You've got nice feet, she says.

Do you think so?

Yes. Smooth. And your toes. I like your toes.

Well, you know, they're just toes.

You say nothing for a while. You watch as Claire works the suds into your skin and between your toes.

It's easy to lose touch, you say at last.

I know it is.

And after what happened –

I know. I agree.

I'm just saying.

Claire gets up and goes into the kitchen again. She returns with a towel.

So tell me more about this man, you say.

There's nothing to tell.

Oh, come off it. Did he remain naked, for instance? Was he fit?

I didn't look at him that way.

Oh, Claire.

I didn't. I really didn't. And no, he didn't stay naked. I

went shopping for him in the morning. I found myself thinking about all kinds of things – when he was here. Things I hadn't thought about before.

Oh yeah.

Not like that. I've said. I didn't think of him like that. All my thoughts were … I don't know … pure. Yes, I suppose my thoughts were pure.

And you are really telling me that nothing happened between you?

I looked after him. He was grateful to me.

Oh, Claire.

You weren't there.

How long did he stay here then?

Not long.

How long?

I can't remember.

A day?

It was more than a day.

A week?

He wasn't well. He needed to rest. He was weak. He needed building up. You can't rush the process. It takes time.

So more than a week?

It may have been.

Didn't you think he'd be better off in a hospital? He might have had something seriously wrong with him.

It never occurred to me. It was funny, but it was like a calling. I knew from the moment I saw him that he had chosen me to bring him back to full health. He liked me reading stories to him. He loved the food I cooked him. He loved me to bake bread for him and –

He's not gone, has he?

What?

He's still here. That's who the bread is for.

Of course not.

Tell me the truth, Claire.

He's not here anymore. He's gone.

So if I was to get up now and walk into your bedroom, I wouldn't find him lying on the bed, would I?

No. I've said. He's gone.

You get up slowly and walk towards the bedroom door. You stand there staring back at Claire, like it's a dare. You put your hand on the knob.

Don't you trust me? says Claire.

Of course I trust you.

Then what are you doing?

You turn the knob.

Just having a look round, that's all.

You stare back at Claire then slowly ease the door open.

Mary.

You freeze at the threshold of the door. It's ajar about an inch.

Okay, you win.

You close the door and walk back across the room.

I'm not calling you a liar. I'm just finding this all just a bit on the weird side.

I knew you would. That's why I didn't want you to know.

You sit down. You take your glass and lean back in the chair. You stare at the ceiling.

What's that? you say, pointing at what looks like a butterfly.

It's been there for weeks.

Is it dead?

No. But it's not moved.

What's it doing there?

I don't know.

Maybe it's going to change into something.

Don't be silly. Butterflies have already changed into something.

Oh, yes, of course. I thought for a moment –

You daft sod.

You both laugh again.

You'd think though, that they would.

And what would they change into?

I don't know. A flower perhaps.

And you're worried about *me*.

Oh, what the hell. Fuck it. It's good to see you, Claire, whatever. It's good to see you. You always were an odd fish though. I could never work you out. I think that's why I liked you. You were a puzzle I had to solve. And you always surprise me. Always. Like that day –

You've said.

But I'm just saying –

You've said.

You sit in silence again. The room has darkened and the smoke from your cigarette has created a fine mist.

Shouldn't you be getting your train?

I suppose so. You look at your watch. Ah! Looks like I've missed it.

What will you do?

There's another one in two hours. I'll stay till then if you don't mind. Do you mind?

No, of course not.

I do like you.

I know.

Just not in that way, that's all.

Okay, Mary. Fucking hell, I think you've made your point.

You stand up. You pace over to the window. You stare out for a while and then go into the kitchen. The bread has cooled. You take a knife and go to cut into it.

What are you doing?

It's ready. I'm starving. You don't mind, do you?

I just don't want you to eat it. Okay? There's some food in the fridge.

Why can't we eat this?

Because I just don't. I just don't. It's my bread. It's mine. I made it. I kneaded it. I baked it. And I don't want you to touch it.

You put the knife back in its block.

Tell me the truth, you say.

About what?

He's here, isn't he? He's in your bedroom now, isn't he? And that bread's for him, isn't it?

And if he was?

So he is?

You stare into Claire's eyes again. So strange and so familiar.

I'll open the door, you say.

Go on then.

You walk over to the bedroom door again. You take hold of the knob and gently turn it. You push the door open just a fraction.

Don't, Mary.

Tell me the truth.

You push the door so that there's a head-sized gap.

Okay. Yes. He's here. You're right. He's in my bed and he's sleeping. Are you satisfied now?

You go over to your wine and gulp it down. You stare out of the window again. Traffic. People. Shops. An old woman with a Pomeranian. A man and a child, hand in hand.

I want you to get rid of him, you say.

What would you say if I told you I was going away. That this might be the last time you see me? How would you feel about that?

That's a funny question.

I'm not laughing.

I don't know how to answer it.

I'm going away.

But you'll come back.

I'm not coming back.

You turn away from the window. You are momentarily blinded. The light of day has stained your retina. The room is dark and full of smoke.

Look, you're here now, and he's in there, and I want you to get rid of him.

I can't.

Why not?

He's sleeping.

Then wake him up.

I can't.

Why not?

He's ill. He needs to get well.

Ring an ambulance. They can take him to a hospital.

I –

Claire! You'll do this or I'll burst in there now and do it myself.

Please, sit down. Have some more wine. You can have some of the bread if you want.

Claire stands up and goes over to the bread. She takes the knife and cuts it into thick slices. She butters it and takes some cheese from the fridge. She puts the bread and the cheese on a plate and places it on the table between you.

Go on, try some.

You stare at the bread, watching the butter melt and sink under the surface.

Please. Just try some.

You take a slice of the bread and bite into it.

Well?

Look, I want you to promise me you're going to get rid of him.

I promise.

I'm going to stay here until you do.

I'm not waking him up.

But he will wake up, won't he?

Of course he will … soon … I should think. He's nearly recovered.

But what's wrong with him?

I'm not a doctor, Mary. I don't really know.

You don't seem to know anything about him.

There's a good reason for that.

Is there?

Yes.

But, I mean, you don't even know his name, do you?

I don't think it matters.

But why not? Why don't you know his name, for Christ's sake?

He's lost his memory.

Oh, come off it. People don't really lose their memory. That's just in books.

That's just in films. People in real life don't do that.

Of course they do. If you're concussed enough, you lose your memory. It's a recognised medical condition.

Look. I've had enough of this. I've been waiting ages now for him to wake. And if you don't go in there and wake him, I will. I mean it, Claire. I've reached the end of my tether with you.

He should be waking up soon.

You get to your feet. You're right, you say. He's waking up right now.

Okay, stop! I'll do it. Only, I want to tell you something first.

So tell me.

There's something I've not told you about me.

So what is it?

Sit down.

I don't want to sit down. Just tell me what it is.

Listen. What happened in that club that time –

I'd like to apologise for that. I was –

It's me who should apologise.

I went too far, I shouldn't have –

I was E'd up. And, and … I was emotional. You just looked so fucking cool. And gorgeous. I was treating you like I've been treated. By blokes, I mean.

It was out of order, but I was out of order, so we're quits.

I wanted to see how it felt. I wanted to feel how they felt.

Look, the reason why I slapped you … It wasn't because, I don't know, but it wasn't because I didn't, you know, like it. I did. Only, I mean, it was a club. There were people there, Claire, people I knew.

I'm not a dyke.

Neither am I.

I just wanted you to know that.

It's settled. Now come on, let's get rid of this bloke. I'm not going until we do.

But, it's not as simple as –

I'm not messing, Claire. I mean it.

But, you don't understand.

Just get in there now.

But –

You open the door and push Claire in. You stand outside waiting. You pace the room. You go over to the window again. The light of day seems even brighter now, the room darker and foggier. You wait a few minutes. You listen. You can hear some moving about but not much else.

How long are you going to be in there?

I'm coming.

It can't take that long to wake him up. I'm going to come in there myself if you don't bring him out.

Nearly ready.

Come on.

I want to say something first.

So say it.

I forgive you.

What?

I said, I forgive you.

Forgive me for what? I don't want your forgiveness. Just get out here now.

The door opens and Claire appears. Only now she is the man. She is naked from the waist up. Her hair is wet and combed back into a mane. You laugh out of shock.

Stop mucking about, Claire.

Claire walks slowly towards you.

Who's Claire?

Pack it in, you're freaking me out.

I don't have a name. Do you want to give me a name?

How about 'headcase'?

Claire walks towards you, until she is just a few feet away. She lets the sheet that was wrapped around her waist drop. And slowly you take her in your arms again.

ALREADY MORNING

You want a pub, but there are no pubs, just saunas. If you want to get drunk you have to take your clothes off. It is fun at first but after a while, you just want to have a drink with your clothes on. You are living in a flat attached to a house, in some remote village in the south. The nearest town is Varnamo. You are living with a Swedish woman called Anna. You met her in a nightclub in England and somehow ended up here. The house is her parents'.

Anna is working in a primary school earning the only money either of you have, cleaning the floors and waxing them. You are not able to work. The government is cracking down on illegal immigrants and there are public information films warning farmers not to hire Turks, or any other foreigners.

There is a Western theme town about thirty miles out called High Chaparral, built by an eccentric Swedish tycoon. You went to see it one day out of sheer boredom. Mock saloons with people paid to pretend they were shoeing horses. Men in Stetsons chewing gum, talking in what they thought was an American accent. And yet there was more life here than you had seen so far in Sweden. There was a stagecoach and you took a ride in it. A gang of outlaws overtook it and pretended to hijack it. You had to pretend to be scared as they pretended to be bad, and you don't know who was the worst at it. It gave you an idea though, that you could work there, you could do a good John Wayne impersonation, hang around looking like an extra from some film set. Easy money.

The evenings are the worst. Her dad, Nils-Alan, is an alcoholic. He has a dark room where he disappears for hours 'developing'. He reappears later, his eyes all over the place, trying to persuade you to join him in the sauna. What's better, you sometimes go along with it, sit, skin turning lobster pink, supping warm Swedish lager. Some evenings, he plays you his collection of Swedish jazz, expounding his theory of what constitutes music: music must contain three elements – reethum, melodee and… There is something else but you can't remember. You talk about the Western theme town. He likes the idea of you working and he wants to help you get a job. He asks around at work for a pair of cowboy boots and a Stetson.

Things between you and Anna aren't really working out. It's no one's fault, you have been creatures of the evening, facial features unblemished in the dim lighting: late night bars, clubs every night, drinking, dancing, finding dark secluded corners. She has idealised you and you have idealised her, and it is a bit of a shock: the sober dawn.

Her mum, Majbrit, has a bike, one of those collapsible shoppers. You borrow it and take a ride at midnight. You are surrounded by countryside, only there is no access to it. It is all lakes and forest. But the forest is too densely planted to work a path through, and you haven't yet mastered walking on water, so bike it is. You ride about twenty miles or so. It is flat and there are dynamo lights attached to the wheels. You ride into a moose. It is huge. Its eyes light up in the dim light of the dynamo bulb. Red pupils. You have built up some speed and it is only yards away. Next, you are flat on your back, the bike on its side, some distance from you, the moose looking down at you with a dazed expression.

A few days later Anna's dad comes home from work all excited. He's got the gear. There is a pair of steel-tipped boots, leather chaps, a black waistcoat, denim shirt with silver collar tips, boot lace tie and the obligatory Stetson. You get Anna to ring up, ask about jobs. There is a vacancy for a stable hand. There are quite a few locals going for it but you think you'll be in with a chance. You practise your John Wayne impression in Majbrit's full-length mirror. You have the talk and the walk and the cocksure grin.

On the morning of the interview, you set off a few hours before, as you have no transport other than Majbrit's shopping bike, which only has one gear, and tiny wheels. The interview is at nine, so you set off at six to be on the safe side. It is windy and you find the cycling tough. Your leather chaps flap like wings. Your Stetson is fluttering behind you in the breeze, tied around your neck with a piece of string. You have borrowed a red-and-white polka dot bandana from Majbrit and it is cushioning your throat from the tension of the hat strap.

You get there far too early. It is locked up and there is no one around. It is cold so you cycle round in circles to keep warm. You have put plenty of deodorant on before setting off, but now your own body odour is starting to overpower it. Your back is wet with sweat, and the wind feels cold as it travels over it. You wait for an hour before the doors open. There is already a queue outside the boss's office. You chain up the bike outside the stables next to a horse's watering trough. A cowgirl is dragging a brush through the matted mane of a stallion. You wink at her and give her your best John Wayne smile. She looks away.

You join the other hopefuls at the back of the queue. They all have similar outfits, though some haven't made much of an effort, just the boots, jeans and a denim shirt, not that different from what they would wear to the pub, if there was such a thing at that time, in that part of Sweden. The queue slowly diminishes, as each one in turn steps into the office and gives their impersonation. You have yours ready, saying it over and over in your head: get off your horse and drink your milk, get off your horse and drink your milk, get off your horse and…

Next!

You ride the thirty miles back, the wind ruffling your Stetson and your bootlace tie, chaps flapping once again. You didn't get the job: your John Wayne wasn't as convincing as a Swedish John Wayne. The man wanted to know why you would milk a horse. You tried to explain that this is a quote from a film, but something is lost in translation. It is decision time that night. Anna has just found out that her granddad is terminally ill. He's been diagnosed with a tumour on his brain. He only has a few weeks to live. His name is Valdemar and it is his eightieth birthday. You have no money; Anna has a little from the cleaning job, but you have nothing, not even enough for a loaf of bread or a stamp to send word of your whereabouts back home to England.

It is agreed, there and then. Anna will go and see her granddad and you will go with her. He lives several hundred miles away, up north, in a place called Falkoping – a big town with modern facilities. Anna's brother lives in Stockholm which isn't that much further; you can stay with him after, make a proper trip out of it. You pack.

The next day you go into Varnamo. You want to get something to show your gratitude to Majbrit and Nils-Alan. You borrow some notes off Anna. You look for a record for Al, but there is only one record shop. You want John Coltrane, but they don't have any. They can order it, but it will take two weeks. You settle on *A Kind of Blue*, something with melodee and reethum. You get Majbrit some Fiji body lotion, because that's all there is that you recognise.

When you get back, it is still early afternoon. Al is off work. He has been doing some decorating. He has wallpapered the bedroom but has left the space behind the radiator. He says he is going to drain the water out and disconnect it. You say that it would be easier to do it the English way – leave it as it is. But he is unconvinced. I want to do it proplee, you know. So you help him disconnect it.

After three hours struggling and saying sheet! very loud, he finally gives up and settles on the English way. By this point he has already marked the new, white wallpaper with a black spot which he has made with a hammer (he got a bit carried away). He turns the water back on. Although he has not managed to loosen the flange on the radiator, he has managed to break the seal. A stream of water pours out all over the new wallpaper and the carpet. He runs quickly to the mains, which is at the other side of the house, screaming: sheet! sheet! at the top of his voice.

He rings the plumber, who says he is coming at 6pm to replace the seal. It is gone eight before he finally arrives. It gave you some satisfaction to note your different nations are united in this one particular insufficiency.

You eat together, presenting Majbrit and Nils-Alan with your gifts. They are genuinely touched and Maybrit even cries when she unwraps the paper concealing her Fiji body lotion. That night you all watch *Wish You Were Here* on the one terrestrial TV channel available. It featured Bath, St Ives and Land's End. You will never see her parents again.

Valdemar's eightieth birthday party consists of just you, Anna and a neighbour, a frail old lady who has baked a cake. Anna has bought him his favourite chocolates. You agree to polish his shoes as he isn't well enough to do it himself. He hasn't seen Anna for months but only manages a weak half-smile. He doesn't speak any English; his second language is German, like all his pre-war generation. You nod to each other instead.

It is a small flat. The sofa converts into a bed – that is where you will sleep. Valdimir is in bed by nine. He has struggled to last till then. There is no light in his eyes. He looks like a man who has reached the end and gone past it. It is a kind of after-life he is in now where he just remains. Anna is tired too, all the travelling. You make the sofa into a bed and dress it with the bedding from the hall cupboard.

She is asleep and you are wide awake, thinking about what you are going to do. You can't stay in Sweden. You and Anna are over, only she doesn't know it yet. You take another beer from the fridge and go and sit out on the balcony.

It is a post-war tenement. You are two floors up. Each flat

has a balcony that is twinned with its neighbour. Structurally, there is only one balcony for two flats – each balcony divided by a frosted glass partition. You sit on a deck chair looking up at the sky. It is still light. The sun has gone, leaving the clouds burning with gold and pink. You feel like you are in two entirely different places, both on the balcony of the second floor flat in some suburb of Falkoping, and also up there in the blazing haze of sunset, strung out across the dying fire of dusk.

You can go back to England – but to what? You have nowhere to live, no money, no job. You can go across to Germany perhaps. You have friends there and you can stay with them, but for how long? You can hear Valdemar snore. It's a gentle hypnotic sound. He seems to have more to say asleep than he does awake. You picture his face. His grey flesh stretched across his bones. The thin strands of hair combed across his bare head. His eyes sunken in their sockets, as though retreating – as though his face had given up concealing the skull beneath. Is this what you are avoiding? The slow ebb?

You can hear voices down below. Swedish voices, a man and a woman. They are shouting and laughing. You stand up and walk over to the rail. Peer down. There is a man with a big moustache and mullet hair, sitting astride the shoulders of a woman, a Brunhilde with Wagnerian peroxide locks and a scuffed denim jacket. She staggers from side to side as he tries to guide her over to the balcony of the flat next door. She falls over and he totters to the floor. They collapse in a heap of giggles. They are drunk.

When he spots you, he stands up and shouts. You know very little Swedish, just managing to communicate that you can't understand him. Ah! Ingleesh! He seems pleased. He explains that they have been to a friend's house but that they have locked themselves out. The keys are on the coffee table. He asks if you will climb across and let them in? Of course you will. Why not?

The flat could not be more different to Valdemar's. It is all the colours of the rainbow. There are garish murals on the walls of Western scenes. There are posters advertising Wild West films. *The Magnificent Seven*, *The Wild Bunch*, and a poster of Elvis, as Jess Wade in *Charro!* They have a white sofa with pink fur cushions. Behind this there is a table with an aquarium and a turquoise plastic fountain. It has beads of glue-like liquid dripping down fine threads of fishing line. There are little lights which light up the dewy pearls of crystal as they descend into pools of sparkling blue, encrusted with pink and turquoise shells and gold pebbles. You pick up the keys from the coffee table and let them in. They are so grateful that they insist you stay for a drink. You sit down on the sofa next to the fountain.

You drink Jack Daniels. They know the High Chaparral very well, know the owner personally. He always gets them in free. There is a club there in the evenings and they have spent many a night line dancing. It seems a long way to go for a night out, but then again, there doesn't seem to be anywhere else. You give them your John Wayne impression, which they think is very good. It is nice at last to be acknowledged. They laugh. They ask you to do it again.

You laugh all night, they find what you say funny, and you laugh at what they say also, as their faces are smiling and they seem to expect it. In truth, you understand very little of what they are saying, and you suspect this is true for them also, of what you say in return.

You finish off the bottle and start on some lager. They are a sweet couple, bringing each other into the conversation all the time, helping each other when one can't find the right English word. This leads to little side debates in Swedish as they try to find the exact translation. Then they smile at each other and continue with the conversation. You are fascinated by how harmoniously they seem to co-exist. Each anticipating the other's needs. A cigarette. A drink. Finishing off each other's sentences, laughing out of genuine amusement at each other's jokes. They are at ease with themselves and their place in the world. There is something truly alive in their delight of the moment.

It is early in the morning when you say your goodbyes. You have one last laugh, as now *you* are locked out. You have to climb back over the balcony. You take this slowly, as your head is spinning and your co-ordination poor. You slide open the glass doors and make your way across to the makeshift bed. Anna is asleep, her body completely relaxed, head far back on the pillow, mouth slightly agape. She looks beautiful. You remember meeting her that first night, seeing her with her friends on the dance floor, the first time your lips touched.

You lie down on top of the sheets, careful not to wake her. The moon is out and its silver rays slither through the gaps in the blinds. In the morning you will tell her you are leaving. And it is already morning.

MANN

Mann pressed the switch which connected two metal plates, allowing an electrical current to flow from the battery of the car, which powered a tiny motor. This motor turned and the window on the driver's side door wound down. Neurotransmitters activating receptors across synaptic clefts, connecting neurons in his brain, triggered muscles in his mouth and jaw. Another set of neurotransmitters triggered an intake of air. This intake was just enough to propel, pneumatically, the spent chewing gum on Mann's tongue at a trajectory and force sufficient to clear the body of Mann's car. Mann swallowed excess saliva, the glottis contracting so that it shut off the trachea, allowing the liquid mixture to travel down Mann's oesophagus.

He was getting annoyed. It was too hot to be stuck in a jam. Roadworks probably. So annoying to be driving at 9.10am and to still find the roads blocked. Everyone should be in work, for Christ's sake, that was why he had deliberately left late. The temperature indicator on Mann's dashboard was rising. It had passed the halfway mark – why hadn't the fan kicked in? He had specifically instructed the garage to re-align the thermostat so it clicked over at the halfway mark. He'd have to take it in yet again, for fuck's sake. He was going to be late for his meeting.

It was now 9.23am. He could make time up once he hit the motorway. The meeting was at 9.45am. If he could get to the junction by 9.30, which was feasible as it was less than 200 yards up the road – although the traffic hadn't moved now for over 3.5 minutes – arriving at 9.44 was not unreasonable. He could do 100mph on the motorway, which meant he could cover the sixteen miles required in ten minutes, just allowing him four minutes to get from the turn-off to the car park.

But now it was 9.25am, and he'd moved only inches, and the dial on the temperature indicator was rising. If he got to the junction at 9.32 he would have to do 117mph to cover sixteen miles in eight minutes, which was pushing it, but was just about possible depending on the flow of traffic. There shouldn't be too much on at this time.

He'd argued with Helen that morning. She didn't understand the pressure he was under at work. The targets. The performance mapping. The competition from younger members of the sales team. She always wanted him to talk about it. As if that would make it go away. But he didn't want to talk about it. It was bad enough being there in the first place without having to describe each agonising detail.

Christ, it was now 9.34am and he'd only gone another few yards. He couldn't possibly be expected to go faster than 120mph which would mean he would not cover the sixteen miles in six minutes. He'd have to make up the time between the turn-off and his destination. What about the speed cameras? There were speed cameras along that stretch. He would have to take the risk, hope there was no film in the box.

Just what the fuck was going on? He drove over to the middle of the road to see if he could see how far the tail-back went. There seemed to be about twenty yards of cars and then it thinned out. The traffic was definitely moving – he'd done about another ten yards – so at this rate he should be at the front by 9.36am at the latest. He'd really have to bomb it, though, to make it. The temperature indicator was about three quarters of the way up and still no fan was clicking on. The bastards hadn't even touched it – it wasn't working at all. It was going straight back to the garage. Why did nothing ever work? Why couldn't you trust anyone to do a job? What was wrong with this country? It was on its knees, with con-men and thieves crouched at every corner, waiting to pounce on you and beat you to a pulp.

He was going to be late. His shirt was wet through. Beads of sweat were running along the creases on his forehead, running down his eyebrows, slipping down the side of his face, trickling down his neck, soaking into his already sweat-drenched collar. They'd argued the day before as well. This time over money. What was it with her? As soon as he had change out of a fiver she was planning ways to spend it. They needed a new sofa, the old one was past it and she'd seen a nice one in a shop in town. They did not need a new sofa, they didn't need a fucking new sofa, there was nothing wrong with it. What was this need she had for replacing perfectly good stuff with new stuff? Just because it wasn't the latest style, just because she'd seen a different one on the telly. All this keeping up all the time, all this competition. He was boring, you have to change things, you just have to. No you don't, you don't have to fuck about with something if it does a perfectly good job. What's boring about a bit of sense, about making sense for a change instead of rattling off all this fucking commercial shit? Shit materials, shit products, shit. Nobody gives a fuck about workmanship. What about pride in what you do instead of trying to rip everyone off all the time? Try that for a change instead of fighting over crap. Try thinking straight instead of spouting all that.

Christ, it was so hot. He had the windows wound down but there was no breeze because the car was hardly moving. He must be as hot as the car's engine. He could feel his feet squirm in his shoes. His groin was grimy with the slime of his perspiration. He was going to give them what for. Just what the fuck were they playing at? He'd get that cocky mechanic bastard and lock him in his office. Then he'd turn up the heating and watch him sweat through the window. Keep moving it up until he was passing out. Cook the fucker in his own juices. Keep on going till he was dead. Yeah, he'd kill him. He'd had enough of being ripped off. What would Helen say then when he told her he'd killed the man at the garage? Do you want to talk about it? No, he did not want to talk about it. How many years would he get? How bad is prison anyway? At least it's cool, at least you get fed. No fucking bosses on your back. No meetings to get to. No bills no wife no cars no phone no ties no suits no…

It was now 9.45. That's it, they would be starting it. We'll have to start without Mann, they'd say. We can fill him in when he gets here. It doesn't bode well, though, does it? And they'd all look at each other in that way and get a pat on the back off the manager. He was so hot now he felt sick. Why didn't anything ever work out? He would have rung but his mobile was on the blink. The one day he needed it. The one time he absolutely relied on it. And there was nothing. He was stuck, drowning in his own sweat.

He was approaching the end of the queue. Cars were driving wide as though around something. There must be something in the road, but he'd passed no roadworks sign. Perhaps something had fallen off a load and was blocking the lane. He could see a shape now through the window of the car in front. A large object on the tarmac. As he approached he could make it out. It was a body, a human body, lying across the road. As he got closer he saw that it was a man, lying with his left cheek pressed against the concrete. The eyes staring up at him were crying.

What was wrong with the man? Why was he crying? And why had he decided to do this in the middle of the road? Didn't he realise he could get killed? Or was this what he was trying to achieve? If it was, he was making a mess of it. Of all the ways to kill yourself, why this? Didn't he realise the hell he was making of people's lives? Didn't he know people's jobs were at stake, that people's health, people's livelihoods were being jeopardised just because he'd had enough?

Couldn't he have swallowed some pills, dangled from the rafters, or jumped off a multi-storey car-park? For God's sake, get a grip of yourself. Life was shit for everyone, but they didn't all go and top themselves. Sure, it was the easy way out, but that wasn't the way to go about things, always looking for the easy way out. Besides, there were things to look forward to. It didn't always rain, sometimes the sun came out. You had to make things happen. Plan for things, have things to look forward to on the horizon.

He'd booked a holiday for September, two weeks off. Helen had sorted it out. They were going to Florida, and he couldn't wait. They'd argued at the time, of course. He didn't see why they couldn't just get a cheap package deal to Spain. The main thing was the time off. The sun and the relaxation. It didn't matter where. Of course he fancied the idea of Florida, but really they couldn't afford it. It was spending money they hadn't got. And anyway, what did Florida have that Spain didn't?

The man was right in front of him now, the only thing stopping him from keeping his appointment. The man was staring up at him, the tears flowing freely over his nose and splashing on the hot tarmac. He was roughly the same age and build as Mann. It occurred to him to not go round the body, but instead, to drive over it, to crush his head beneath the wheel of his vehicle. It was what he wanted, and would end the traffic jam.

The car behind beeped at Mann. He realised he'd stopped. If he slammed his foot down now, the man wouldn't even feel anything. But what would happen to Mann? It would be manslaughter, surely. And what would he tell them at the garage when they asked why his tyre tread was clogged with human brain?

As he drove around the man, he wondered if he should stop and have a word with him instead. See if he could talk him out of it. But no one else had, they'd all just driven past. Perhaps that was the best thing to do, after all. Of course he'd missed the meeting now, not that it really mattered. What did he care what people thought about him? Commission rates, projected figures – it was all meaningless. It was all just crap. He built up some speed and a soft breeze travelled across him. He overtook the car in front once he got on the motorway, first in the fast lane, then back to the middle again, behind a lorry. He looked over at the temperature dial. It was returning to normal. He was still wet with sweat but it was no longer hot. It was cool.

Mann looked up at the sun beaming down on him. There were clouds surrounding it, but not thick enough to obscure it. A perfect orange disc. What an incredible thing the sun was. Really it was. Always there staring down at the Earth. It occurred to him at that moment for the first time, that the sun was God. The sun staring down now was the eye of God peering at him. It had always been looking at him without him realising. It had seen him being born. It had seen the birth of everyone, without blinking. Why hadn't he realised? Why hadn't anyone else realised? All these people packing into churches to speak to their creator. How ridiculous it seemed now. Not knowing that it was there, outside, the life source, all along. Looking at everyone throughout all time, throughout all existence.

Mann felt strangely reassured by this. He felt calm. And he drove his Alpha AB into the back of the BA Logistics articulated truck.

THE MAN IN THE WHITE COAT

Outside it is snowing. The snow already covers the lawn in the back garden, and the tops of the walls. You go to the doormat, but the post hasn't been yet. You pour yourself a bowl of Frosties and watch the Chuckle Brothers on television. You put the empty bowl in the sink, grab your school bag and close the front door softly behind you, careful not to wake your dad.

You are thirteen years old today. Your mum and dad split up six months ago. Partly it was a relief. No more arguing, no more fighting, no more throwing things. The house is quiet now. You see her every weekend, for ice skating, ten pin bowling, or Pizza Hut with her and her new boyfriend, Damian. He is ten years younger than her and tattooed. You do this to keep the peace.

You feel your mum has betrayed you. Damian works for some club in town called Rio's. He's a sound and lighting man. She moved in with him straightaway. She packed her bags one day and Damian pulled up in his banana-coloured MG sports car. Off they went, music blaring out of the speakers.

Christmas. Just you and your dad. You were invited to Damian's place, by your mum, but you wanted to stay with your dad. Your dad has cooked a chestnut roast instead of a turkey as he's recently turned vegetarian, although the sprouts and roast veg are the same. He lets you have a small glass of wine with your meal. You gulp it down. It goes straight to your head. You feel like you are floating. You win a green plastic angel in your cracker. Your dad, a pink plastic hair grip. You both wear your coloured tissue paper crowns and tell each other jokes. You laugh. Your dad quietly sighs.

Your mum has bought you an iPod and your dad has bought you a hooded top.

Thanks, Dad, it's cool, you say.

Do you like it?

Course I do, Dad. It's great.

You're not just saying that?

No, Dad, course not. Like I say, it's cool.

Though not as good as your iPod, I bet.

Your father's eyes are watering and you're embarrassed. You take your fork and you shovel in a mouthful of chestnut roast. You swallow and take another mouthful. Your dad doesn't look up. Drips of water from his eyes are landing on the carrots. You hand over the iPod.

I don't really want this, Dad. You can have it.

Your dad doesn't speak. He gets up and leaves the room. When he returns he seems more composed. He takes the half-empty bottle of wine from the middle of the table.

Want another, Son?

Are you sure, Dad?

Sod it, it's Christmas.

He fills up both your glasses. You watch the *Doctor Who* Christmas Special on TV. For some reason, this makes your dad cry again. You wish you could comfort him, but putting your arm round him doesn't feel right somehow, and you can't think of the right thing to say.

On the television there's a killer Christmas tree, with its arms spinning, approaching the Doctor's assistant, Rose, her mother, and her boyfriend. They're recoiling in horror. It should be funny, but it's not, it's sinister. A distorted Christmas carol plays in the background. It sounds demented.

You remember being six, waking up at four o'clock, Christmas morning. It's still dark and you approach the bag at the bottom of your bed with some trepidation. But there's no need to worry – Santa has been. You drag the bag into your parents' room. They wake bleary-eyed. Dad switches on the bedside lamp.

Morning, Son, has he been?

Yeah. He's left me loads of presents.

That's 'cos you've been a good boy. Bring it up here. I'll help you open them.

Your mum puts her dressing gown on and goes down to the kitchen to make some breakfast. Your dad helps you unwrap the parcels. They seem to glow with their own light. They seem both heavier and lighter than you imagined them to be. The paper gets torn and scattered all over the bedroom. On the bed are books, games, clothes, videos and action toys. You told the teacher at school you didn't believe in God, but you believe in Santa. You're looking at the evidence.

Your mum has come into the room with a tray. She puts it down on the floor. She's cooked you fried tomato, sausage, bread, scrambled egg and toast. You each have your own glass of fresh orange juice. Your mum and dad have hot mugs of tea.

Be careful not to spill that.

She hands you the drink. You put it by the side of the bed, too excited yet to take a sip. She hands a plate and a mug to Dad. He gulps from the mug, then puts it, steaming, on the bedside cabinet. He harpoons a sausage and dips it in the mustard.

Cheers, love, it looks lovely.

Afterwards you all have a hug. The room is warm and cluttered with brightly coloured wrapping paper. Your mum is smiling. She kisses you on the cheek. You remember that Christmas.

The next Christmas your father isn't there. You want to know where he's gone, but all your mum will tell you is that he's away. He isn't well, and he'll be back soon.

You feel a lump in your throat. You turn back to the television. They're all stood outside the Tardis now. It's parked in the midst of a concrete tenement. When Rose says goodbye to her mother and her boyfriend, to go with the newly-regenerated Doctor, your dad shakes with emotion.

We don't have to watch this, Dad. Should I put something else on?

Your dad doesn't answer. He covers his eyes with his hands. His cheeks are damp. You're relieved when the theme tune starts and the credits appear.

It's five weeks since that Christmas day. Your dad's progress has been patchy. Some days he seems to cope. He'll smile at you and say: we're all right me and you, Son, aren't we? But other days, he seems unreachable, or worse, staring out as though there were some monster coming towards him.

You do your best not to worry him. You make sure you always come straight home from school. Your dad's a picture framer and has converted the garage into a workshop. In the middle is a large table and on the floor, the remnants of framing material, off-cuts of wood and resin moulds.

You always go straight to the workshop. Want a cuppa, Dad?

Sometimes your dad will be at work, gluing, sawing or drilling. But other times he's staring into space, or sat with his head in his hands, sawdust staining his work clothes.

What…? Oh, yeah, a cuppa. Thanks.

When the school bell rings at half past three, you're glad. You don't mind school. You wish there wasn't so much mucking about in class from some of the kids, and you wish the work the teachers set was more interesting, but apart from that, it's okay. Today has been odd. You mentioned your birthday only a few days ago to your mate Liam, and you're surprised he hasn't remembered.

As you walk up Springhead Road, where you live, you think that at least the post will have been by now. There's bound to be something off your aunty Laura or your uncle Andy. You walk round to the back of the house. Pop in on your dad first, check he's okay. Only, when you get to the garden gate, you're startled by what you see.

There, in the middle of the snow-covered lawn, is a television sitting on top of a suitcase. How strange it looks there, marooned on the battered luggage, adrift in the white foam of snow. You open the garden gate and walk across, the snow scrunching under the soles of your school shoes. You walk right up to the object and circle it a few times. You reach a finger out and touch it. It's real. You stare at it. At last you press the button at the bottom left-hand corner of the set, and, miraculously, the glass screen lights up.

It's the news. Only not the news as you've seen it before. A man in a white lab coat sits behind a desk, and he's wearing over-sized, red-coloured spectacles. He holds a piece of paper in front of him and is reading from it.

So, you think this is weird? Wait till you see what's inside.

The man stares out at you. He rustles the paper and then repeats his message. You're puzzled. You walk to the external door of the workshop. You open it and enter. Inside is the usual array of off-cuts, tools and sawdust, but no dad. You're so used to seeing your dad, on entering the room, that you're taken aback, unnerved even. Your dad works with the radio on, but today there's no sound coming from the speaker. You look around, but still no sign of dad. Finally, you go into the internal door which opens into the house.

As you do, you're greeted by loud cheers. You're surrounded by people. Family and friends. Some of them set off party poppers and streams of coloured paper fly up around you. Your dad walks over. He isn't in his work clothes. He's wearing his newest shirt, and some clean trousers.

Did you think I'd forgot?

You don't know what to say. You're confused.

But…

Come on.

Your dad leads you into the living room, which is now decorated with different-coloured balloons and a large banner saying: Happy 13th Birthday Josh. The dining table is full of party food. There's four or five friends from school, and your mum with her boyfriend. They're all smiling at you.

Your dad hands you a parcel.

It's been a bugger keeping this one quiet.

You take the parcel off your dad but are too dazed to open it. Your mum comes over and hands you a present too.

Liam, your friend from school, comes over. I was gonna tell you, but yer dad said not to.

Once the party has settled down, you ask your dad how he's rigged up the television.

He puts his arm around you and leads you out into the garden. You walk over to the contraption. Your dad takes the television off the top of the suitcase. He unzips the suitcase flap. He shows you a power pack and a video player in the suitcase. The video player is on a loop. He's filmed a friend dressed up in the lab coat and glasses with a hand-held camera.

Did you like it?

It's brilliant, Dad.

Well, I thought I needed to make amends for Christmas. And, well, for… Well for just being a bit crap recently.

He gives you a hug. Me and you, we're going to be all right, yeah?

Course we are, Dad.

You go back to the party. Your dad gets himself a lager and you talk to some of your friends. Your mum beckons you over.

Happy birthday, Son.

Thanks, Mum.

Your dad comes back into the room and walks over to your mum.

No hard feelings, love. Do you want a beer?

Go on then.

How about you, Damo, fancy a beer?

Not for me thanks, I'm driving.

Your dad goes back into the kitchen to fetch your mum a can of lager. It feels normal.

Fuckin nutter, this Damian says under his breath.

Don't, Damian. Not in front of Josh.

But he is. You told me that.

Not now.

Your mum is staring at Damian. She turns to you and smiles. There's something not quite right with that smile.

Damian is whispering. But you told me he'd been in the nut house. What else am I supposed to call him?

I'm warning you!

Look, you want your son back, don't you?

Of course I do.

Well, then.

Your dad walks back into the room. He hands the lager to your mum.

There you go. He looks at Damian and then your mum. Everything okay?

Yes, thanks.

You sure?

This Damian strolls across to your dad. How many times you had your brain fried then?

It's got nothing to do with you.

Damian, please, let's just go.

Your mum is pulling on Damian's sleeve, but he doesn't move.

It isn't right. Damian is staring at your dad.

Don't, please. Come on.

Do you think it's normal – a TV on the lawn?

I can look after my son.

Yeah? Damian says.

You can't take much more of this. Leave my dad alone, you shout.

Damian turns to you. His voice softens. Look, Josh, don't you think you'd be happier with yer mum and me? With normal people?

Your mum turns to your dad. Maybe it would be for the best, David. You'll be much better off without the distraction. Don't you think?

Your dad is trembling. Leave. Just leave.

They walk out of the house. Your dad looks around at all the people staring at him. His eyes are protruding and he's shaking. His face is drained of colour. You hold onto your dad's hand.

You all right, Dad?

You usher him over to a chair and help him sit down. The lager has spilt so you go to the fridge to fetch him a new one. You open it and put it in your dad's hand. He stares at it, as though it were a mystery object. The guests say nothing.

Later that night, after everyone has gone home, you look for your dad. He's not in his bedroom or the bathroom. You can't find him anywhere. You go downstairs and look in all the rooms. Eventually, you make your way to the only room you haven't tried, your dad's workshop. Only he isn't there either. Where can he be? Then you see a light through the window. It's the light from the television that is still on the lawn.

Outside now, you see him standing over the set. It's on, and the looped tape is repeating the phrase. So, you think this is weird? Wait till you see what's inside… Your dad is staring at the man in the lab coat. The snow on the grass glows with reflected light. The air is so cold it catches in your throat. You go over to him and put your hand in his large calloused hand.

It's all right, Dad, you tell him. Everything is going to be all right.

He says nothing. His bottom lip is quivering. He keeps staring at the man in the white coat and the over-sized, red-rimmed spectacles. You squeeze his hand hard. You grip on to it with all your might. If you let go he'll drift off, up into the night sky.

THIRD PERSON

She sits on the bench and watches the children play. Long-ingly? It's not certain. He throws a small ball for a medium-sized mongrel dog. Attached to the ball is a rope and handle. With this he manages to throw the ball a great distance. His arms are strong – not big, but long and well-defined. He has slim limbs and dark skin. He is tall, possibly lanky, but this only adds to his boyish attraction, as though the rest of his body were catching up. He is in his late thirties though he walks like a thirteen-year-old boy. Does she notice this? It's not certain. She looks like she could be thinking, but there is no way of knowing if she is. It is more than likely that whatever she is thinking will be of no interest. Nothing of interest could come from that dull head. She has thin mousy hair with a weak wave. Her face is plain, her eyes pale and dim.

They've been here about half an hour. Thirty-three minutes. It is Sunday. They are always here for about half an hour on Sunday – before he leaves her to go to the pub. She goes to see her mother. She is her mother, small and callous. She is at her mother's. He joins her there later for Sunday dinner. They do not speak. They never speak. Not to each other. They have nothing to say. To each other.

He does the pub. In the pub he is with his mates. They make him less attractive. His face twists as he tells the same anecdotes to a familiar audience. He is less him when he is with them. He buys them all drinks. Why does he do this? They buy them back again. He is buying time with pints.

He does not want to do the Sunday in-law thing. He does. He turns up half an hour late. The mother answers the door. She is sat at the table. Waiting. The mother leads him to his chair. An executioner leading a condemned man. She is not happy. He is late yet again. He does not care what she thinks, he is warm with beer. It may even add to his glow that he has annoyed the both of them. She doesn't say anything. She is just staring at him – her abattoir eyes wide on a spring lamb. He'd rather play the fool than the dunce. They are served hard potatoes, boiled vegetables and thick brown gravy. The food is edible but has no real taste. It is washed down with mugs of milky tea. There is no wine. There is no levity. Yet there is no serious thought either. The husband of the mother died of respiratory failure brought on by chronic obstructive bronchitis. He spent his life down the pit. He was about to retire. He was fortunate.

After they have eaten, he clears away the dinner things and washes them in the sink. She sits. The mother sits also. They watch *Songs of Praise* as they discuss the neighbours. He takes a long time to clean the pots, as though he were enjoying it. He isn't. They say how useless he is, typical man, no idea, probably chipped half of them, or left a ring in the pan like your father used to do. He is thinking about work. He will be glad to go back. Mondays always go quick, so much to do. He works in an office. She is looking for a job. Part-time. She isn't wanting a job full-time like last time. Who would her mother talk to then?

It is almost painful, hearing them discuss this later that night in bed. She is telling him off for smoking again. She is afraid he will burn the house down. He doesn't even hear her now, so used is he to her routine. He does not think she needs to spend so much time with her mother. He does not think this is good for her. Or her. She is not going to take any notice of him, she is going to do what she wants. She is. He does not finish his cigarette. He turns off the lamp without stubbing out the butt. She is asleep. He does.

I'm a spider. Not literally of course. I'm not an insect – neither is a spider. I'm a spider because I live in a web. Not an actual web obviously. I'm not strong enough to grip the thread, and am too heavy for the thread to sustain my mass. I live a spider's life. I don't catch flies though. I think flies are filthy creatures, half-digested dog shit in their guts. Don't ask me why I'm a spider – spiders don't answer those sort of questions – besides, I don't ask you why you are you. You just are.

I say I'm a spider but I haven't done anything wrong. All I've done is drive. And park. And wait. I wait where he won't see me and record his passing. I watch him go in – write down the time. I try and guess which room he will enter first. Which light will switch. When he leaves again I write down the time, again. I don't want to hurt him. Never. I want him to devote himself to me, as I have devoted myself to him. I have a hole in my heart, and he's eating away at it. I'm hollow. I'm crying all the time. The truth is I'm out of control.

I can't decide when I'm all right. I'm afraid to go out, to talk to people, in case I slip up, in case they see what is dying inside me. I'm all right, and that lasts for a while, and I think, great I've got this under control. I can think about him and smile, feel warm with the thought of him. But then I'll have the same thought a few minutes later and I'll cave in. The lump rises up from the stomach. The stomach itself is a knot tightening up. The heart is a shell, painfully hollow. The eyes leak – the full waterworks. I know he doesn't love her. She's his habit and he's hooked, but it's not love. She is his ballast. What does she give him? She doesn't give him anything, she doesn't… She's heartless. The bitch takes advantage of him. She knows he's a caring person with deep tender feelings, so she manipulates him. She's so superficial, he's just a commodity to her. She needs a partner to go round to her mum's or out with her friends so she won't feel left out.

He needs love, and lots of it. He's crying out for love, and only I can give it. I'm full of love and he's full of love and I need to get it out of my system. You know how men are, they seem to put up with more than women. They let women

96

get away with more than women let men get away with. They can't see what's put in front of their nose. You have to cut it off and hand it to them on a plate before they even acknowledge it.

I've been watching a comedy show on TV, trying to cheer myself up. On the comedy show are two characters, Ted and Ralph. Ralph is a country squire and owns a mansion with a large estate. Ted is his gardener and caretaker. He lives on his own in a small cottage within the grounds of the estate. His wife died several years ago. He is a quiet, solemn man. Ralph is the beneficiary of his father's fortunes, but feels far too guilty at the inequality he sees all around him to partake in his family's business interests.

He has no stomach for his meat. Ralph loves Ted, but his love is unrequited. Ted is far too meek to do anything, one way or the other. There is nothing funny about this situation. It is a tragedy. Two people who belong to each other, who live with loneliness, whittling away at their sense of self, when they could be sharing each other. What is this doing in the middle of a comedy sketch show? It is a sick joke. I turn it off. I am crying again.

I have been inside their house. While they were out. It's her over everything. There is nothing of him. She won't let him in. I went into their living room. There was a vase of withered glads on the mantelpiece. At the opposite end is a picture of her with him. They are stood together. They are some distance from each other. Behind them is the sea. In front is the beach. They are in-between. They stand in the gap and stare back. He looks sad and trapped. She looks happy in her misery.

I went up the stairs and into the bedroom. The sheets were still crumpled. I could tell where he'd been lying, as there was a larger mark on that side. I strip to my knickers and climb inside. I fit into the hollow he has left. There is plenty of room – he is all around me. I take off my knickers and stroke the sheets. They are smooth and cool. I sniff the furrow in the pillow where his head has been. I can smell his shampoo. Beneath this smell I can smell him. There is a sweetness in his scent.

I have some radio equipment for covert surveillance. I also have a bunch of skeleton keys. I was surprised how easy it was to get hold of them. I had no idea where they'd be. But I knew they were boys' things, as I'd never seen them in girls' magazines. I found them in *Survival* magazine. At the back where all the adverts are. One for a receiving device, complete with fifty easy to fit and conceal remote microphones, or bugs. And then on the next page, beside an advert for a genuine Breton cap, a little sketch of a bunch of keys with a heading which said, these keys will open anything, yours for only £9.99 plus package and posting. I have already bugged her mum's. I did it when she was cleaning. She has a job at the pub every morning 8-10am seven days a week. I used the rest around their house. Under the bed, in the handset of the phone. In the living room. One behind the photo, and one in the hat stand.

I see him at work. His desk is at the other end of the office. When he gets up to go to the break room, I follow him. I stand behind him at the coffee machine. He turns to apologise. He is getting tea. It takes twenty seconds to brew, where the coffee is instant. I smile back. It's okay, you owe me twenty seconds, I joke. I count up all these twenty seconds, two lots every day, ten a week. He has only worked here for ten months. I've been here years. Still, it's over two hours he owes me.

He says there must be a little man inside the machine swilling tea around a teapot. I smile back again. I agree. A trapped man trapped inside a great big ugly machine, reduced to a machine. Good weekend? I ask. Not bad, he says, then thinks about it. No, actually, it was bad, he laughs. Only he and I know how true this is. He doesn't know I know. He shares things with me without even knowing. We are so close now. There are more people in the queue. More women. They eye his behind greedily. Every woman in the office wants to have their way with him. I stand in the way of them, my chest almost pressed into his elbow. He is oblivious.

It seems to me now, as I write this – sitting on my bed past midnight, no sound, no light, save the lamp by the side of the bed – that we are so far apart in space and time. It's like we've never met, are never going to meet, have nothing that we share. And at the same time you are so close to me. If I close my arms you'll be in them. If I close my eyes I can feel your breath on my neck. I have a hunger deep inside. A sort of sick, insatiable appetite. A worm in my gut eating it up bit by bit. The yearning in my heart is unbearable. It is so intense that I don't know how long I can go on. Without you. Why don't you come to me now, this night, while I wait by the lamp light, while I write out my heart with hot hand and feverish desire? They stop the beat of my heart, my thoughts. They hit me in the chest with regret.

What will it take to draw you into my web which stretches across space, across time, which I have spun in my mind in order to stop you from falling into darkness? What bait is needed? I've made such a beautiful pattern with the threads of thought that connect us. I have woven a nest of silk between barren branches on autumn evenings. With my long legs, with my burning flesh, I'll gather you into me. You'll see yourself as you really are for the first time. You'll be you, I'll be me, we'll be we. You will be happy. And me. I will be.

ABOVE AND BENEATH

It was a Tuesday and I was working a late shift when the monkeys took over the hospital. Most of the patients were in bed. I was in the dayroom with Darius playing Scrabble when there was a knock at the window. Actually, more a thud than a knock.

What was that?

I reached across to the curtain and pulled it back. Nothing. Just my own reflection, looking slightly bewildered, and Darius in the distance, looking darker, stooped over the Scrabble board. I put my eyes to the glass. My forehead touched the cold surface. I cupped my hands and peered out. As my eyes adjusted, I could just make out the trees in the distance looking like a line of plump pigeons. The sky was black. I could make out the car park, with three cars; my black Ford Focus, a beaten-up red Allegro and a yellow Mini Cooper, but there was nothing else. No movement. I replaced the curtains.

Darius wasn't on any medication, except for a mild sedative, one he had self-prescribed many years ago and as a courtesy to Darius, the doctor persisted in supplying. In fact, Darius displayed very few characteristics which were 'indicative' of any mental state. He was closed but not pathologically so. He was fastidious, but not obsessive. When I had first started working at the hospital, I had assumed Darius was a nurse, not a patient. It was only three days into my shift that another nurse pointed out his real status. I monitored him for quite some time after that but couldn't find anything aberrant in his behaviour.

I was looking at my sorry set of letters – three Ps, two Bs, a J and a blank – when there was another thud, this time louder and more alarming. I knocked my rack of tiles, spilling a blank onto the table. I went to the window again, pulled back the curtain and cupped my hands. Nothing. I stared out across the car park and over to the line of trees. Something moved. It was too quick to identify. I stared harder. A face appeared at the window. I jumped back, knocking my chair over. My heart began to pump my blood much faster, like I'd drank a double shot of espresso. Darius was looking over at me.

What is it?

I had seen a face. I extended my arm in the direction of the window. Have a look yourself, I said, as I backed further away. Darius walked tentatively across to the curtain. He took the cloth in one hand, paused and then pulled it back. He peered out. For a long time he stood there, just peering.

Do you see anything?

For a moment he ignored me, then he replaced the curtain and walked back to the table. Nothing there, he said, and sat back down. He didn't seem in the least bit disturbed. It's your go.

Even if I had been able to think of a word to place on the board, the idea of continuing with the game was untenable. There was something out there. We'd both heard two loud thuds, I'd seen something move, and I'd also seen a face at the window. I went over to a different window and pulled back the curtain.

Turn the light off, I said to Darius, and he got up and walked towards the door. He flicked off the switch and the outside became clearer.

I could see the cars in detail now and I could see the cracked concrete where they were parked. Something was poking out of the side of the beaten-up Allegro. An arm? A leg? I stared at the object. Then it moved. Next, a shape, a crouched silhouette, skipping across the car park and into the trees. A teenager wearing a hooded top? Then another shape across the far side of the car park, darted out from behind a wall and then into a bush. I stared harder, trying to see beyond the trees and bushes. Whack. A fist on the window. I fell back in shock.

I got to my feet. I looked over at Darius.

It must be those kids again, I said. I'm going to ring the police.

I walked towards the office. Bang, thud, then thud again. They seemed to be hitting the windows simultaneously. I could hear the glass shake in its frame. The doors were triple-locked and the windows were all double-glazed with specially reinforced glass, but they could be broken, I was sure of that. There were four windows in the day room. The largest was the most vulnerable. Mary appeared at the entrance to the corridor, which led to the sleeping quarters.

What's going on? she asked.

She was clinically depressed and on strong anti-depressants. She normally slept through anything.

It's nothing Mary. Go back to bed.

I heard a noise. Outside.

You must have been dreaming.

Why are the lights off?

Bulb's gone. Now go back to bed.

She didn't move, just stood at the hall entrance in her dressing gown, rubbing sleep from her eyes. Thud and then thud, thud, thud. All four windows were hit. The whole building seemed to shake with the impact. Mary looked at me anxiously.

What's out there?

She approached the largest of the windows and peered out. There was a pause, then she screamed and fell. I ran over to her. I helped her up.

Monkeys, she said. There's monkeys, out there.

I shook my head.

Teenagers, if we ignore them, they'll go away.

I hadn't even finished my sentence when there was a succession of thuds. It felt like every window was under siege. I went to the large window, and there it was, a monkey, its face

102

pressed up against the glass, its fists banging on the pane. I could see my car in the distance. There was a monkey squatting on top of it, jumping up and down on the roof. I could see three or four monkeys running across the car park. There must have been eight or nine monkeys in total.

Eric, a paranoid schizophrenic, was standing at the entrance in his pyjamas.

What the hell's going on? he said.

We're under attack, Mary answered. Monkeys everywhere.

Eric took a moment to register this. He went to the large window and looked out. He shook his head.

Oh my god, he said. Look at this.

I walked over to the window. Darius and Mary were standing either side of Eric. They were looking at a monkey who was brandishing a steel bar. He was smashing up the cars with it. He brought it down on my windscreen. Crash, then on the side windows of the Mini Cooper. Crash, crash. Then he ran towards us holding the steel bar aloft.

I just had time to shout, get back! before the monkey smashed the window. I ushered the three of them into the office and locked the door behind me. The office was glass-fronted with single panes, it wouldn't take the monkeys long. I picked up the telephone receiver and dialled 999. As I waited for a connection I witnessed the shards of glass exploding across the dayroom, embedding themselves into the soft furnishings and falling onto the carpet like frozen rage. I was through to the operator.

Monkeys, you say?

Yes, monkeys. You need to bring at least four cars. Make sure they're armed.

As I was talking I saw that the monkey had now entirely demolished the glass and was climbing in. Then another monkey, then another, then another. They lolled and gimped across the room. One of them went over to the big fruit bowl on the table and started to stuff his mouth with an apple. His mate came and joined him, stuffing a banana into his mouth without peeling it. There were five or six monkeys now gathered around the bowl. They finished off the fruit and threw the bowl across the room.

I whispered down the receiver, they're here. In the room. Please be quick. It's the hospital off Longside Lane. I replaced the receiver. I turned to Darius, Mary and Eric and whispered again, be quiet, don't move. If they don't know we're here, they might leave. There were two monkeys urinating over one of the sofas, the amber fonts of urine spattering off the vinyl polymer covering.

The monkeys finished off and shook themselves. Mary nudged the lamp on the office table and it fell with a clatter. The monkeys, as though choreographed, all stopped what they were doing, and looked over at the office. They stared at us, their black eyes inscrutable. I held my breath, as though this might delay their response. A banana smacked the glass. Then a monkey ran at us. The others followed, screeching.

Quick!

I had the filing cabinet and I was dragging it in front of the window. I just managed to cover the pane when the first monkey smashed the glass.

What now?

I was panicking and I couldn't think of a way out. The monkey had his arm in the room now, grasping and grabbing. We were all huddled behind the desk except for Eric, who stood like a sculpture of fear.

Eric! Over here.

But it was too late. The monkey had him by the wrist. Eric was wrenched towards the window. The monkey was pulling his arm. I heard Eric's shirt rip. Then I saw his skin exposed where the tear occurred. Next I heard the nauseating sound of Eric's flesh split. I saw his skin like a torn rag exposing his flesh and sinew, blood spilling onto his shirt and onto the carpet. Then I remembered, there was a trap door under the office, which led into the cellar. I pushed the desk back and pulled away the rug underneath. I pulled at the trapdoor. It wouldn't budge. Darius saw what I was doing and gave a hand. Mary was watching Eric, as his arm was torn from its socket.

The trapdoor was open. Eric's arm was now completely off. Crimson threads and tissues dangled from the gash. The monkey was waving the arm as though it were a baguette. He was half in the room and half out. The filing cabinet fell to the floor with a clatter.

Mary!

She seemed not to be taking it all in. I grabbed her and pushed her through the trap door. Next Darius. As I jumped into the hole, the monkey leapt into the room. Blackness. I felt for the light switch. I fumbled in the dark. Then light. Darius had found it. There was a thud above our heads as the monkey landed on the trapdoor. I shoved my steel-encased pen into the latch. It wouldn't hold for long, but it would slow the monkey down. The cellars were a labyrinth of corridors and tunnels and boiler rooms and storage spaces where all the feral cats slept. At the far end of the cellars was an old coal chute. It was boarded up from the inside, but it was our only way out.

I found the light on my phone and switched it on. I led the way, with Darius behind me and Mary behind him. I could hear the sound of the trapdoor as the monkeys pulled at it.

Come on, run!

The light from my phone lit up the first few feet in front of us. We came to the end of the tunnel. Two eyes staring at us. I could feel the blood surge through my ventricles. Mary gave a shriek. Then we heard a hiss. It was just a cat. I grabbed a lungful of air. There was the coal chute. It was boarded up with a lap panel and some paling, and hammered together with roofing nails. I grabbed at the paling. As I did, I could hear the pen in the latch of the trapdoor snap and the latch bang open. They'd got through.

I worked one of the pales loose and used it to lever up the

rest of the panelling. As I did, I could hear the monkeys' ghastly screeching as it echoed down the corridors. The sound of the monkeys seemed to spur Darius into action and we both tore at the wood. We were almost there, just the thin lap panel in the way now. I turned around to see the faint sickening outline of one of the monkeys at the other end of the tunnel. They had found us.

With one last burst of energy, I shouldered the lap panel, the wood splintering. I banged open the hinged doors of the chute. The monkey was lurching towards us. I reached up to feel the tarmac on my hands. I grabbed the frame of the door and pulled myself out of the tunnel. I grabbed hold of Darius, then Mary. But as I took hold of Mary, the monkey grabbed her ankles. He was much stronger than I was, and I had to let her go. I closed the doors on her and secured the bolt. As I did, I heard her scream.

I looked around. Where to go where they wouldn't find us or outrun us? We could run towards the trees, but that's where they had come from. The only choice we had was the long tarmac driveway leading to Longside Lane; but the monkeys would surely spot us and catch up.

There, in the window frame of the dayroom, where I had stood ten minutes ago watching them demolish my car, was one of the monkeys, his rangy silhouette positioned towards where we were standing. We were caught in his stare. The only choice now was to run for it.

We were about to make the dash when the car park was flooded with headlamps. It was a police car. The monkey spotted it too. He leapt out of the smashed window and skipped towards it. The car pulled up just as the monkey jumped onto the bonnet. As he did, a policeman fired through the windscreen, shooting the animal through the chest. It fell to the ground, dead.

Another police car pulled up, then another. What happened next was a blur. Monkeys and policemen, gunshots and dead bodies. Soon, monkey corpses were lying strewn across the car park. I turned around and hugged Darius, out of relief. He seemed shocked by this intimacy and his arms lay by his side, like an Irish dancer.

That was four months ago now. The hospital has erected metal guards over the windows; just a precaution, they say, the monkeys won't be back. But I can't rest. I sit here fidgeting and watching the windows anxiously. I'm in the dayroom with Darius, playing Scrabble. I've locked the fruit bowl away in the safe, as I now do every shift, and I finger the Manila butterfly knife in my pocket; its cool carbon swedge, brass handle and magnetic latch, warm and reassuring. I'll be ready for them next time, when the monkeys come again.

THE PHONE CALL

Hi, Mum.

Hello, love, I was just thinking about you.

Were you really? What were you thinking about?

I can't remember now, love.

Sorry about yesterday, Mum. It's very high pressured at work at the moment. Happy birthday, Mum.

Thanks, love.

Did you have a nice day?

Oh yes, it was lovely. I was invited to Elma's for tea.

That's nice.

It was, yes.

What did you get then?

Well, Elma got me perfume, and Anne got me some chocolates, and Cath got me a voucher for Marks and Spencers.

Did you get lots of cards?

Oh yes, lots.

Good.

There was an awkward pause.

And you?

What about me?

Are you okay?

I'm fine, Mum. I'm doing really well. I've got a girlfriend, you know.

Have you really, Son, that's nice, what's she called?

Caroline.

That's a nice name. Is she a Catholic?

I don't think so, Mum.

Oh well, Caroline is a nice name. What's she like?

She's really nice, Mum. You'd like her.

I'm sure I would, love. I best get off. I don't want to waste any of your phone bill.

Don't worry about that, Mum. I'm loaded now, you know.

That's nice. I best get off.

Mum.

Yes.

Do you remember when I was young?

Yes, of course.

Do you remember how we used to read to each other?

Yes, how could I forget.

Mum…

Yes love, what is it?

I…

Yes Son, what's on your mind?

I was just going to say…

Go on, what is it?

Happy Mother's Day for tomorrow.

Thank you love, that's nice.

I won't be able to phone you tomorrow.

Never mind.

Or the next day.

That's okay, love.

I've got an important contract at work and I need to go into the office.

You work so hard.

Everybody does.

I'll let you get off.

Mum, don't go.

Oh, I nearly forgot, I got a phone call the other day.

For me?

Yes, for you.

And?

It was from Jamie.

What did he say?

He said he had some important news for you.

What was it?

He wouldn't say.

Why not?

He said he wanted to speak to you himself.

What did you tell him?

Well, I gave him your telephone number and your address. Did I do the right thing?

Yes, Mum. That's fine, but…

You're not in trouble, are you?

Of course not. What makes you say that?

It's just that he sounded, well, a bit urgent.

His phone's at the top of the stairs. He was probably just out of breath, Mum.

Oh, I see. I expect you're right.

Look after yourself, Mum.

And you. You're all right, aren't you?

Of course I am.

Are you eating enough?

Loads. I'm always taking clients out for meals. You wouldn't believe the amount I go through. But it all comes off the tax. That's why companies have these expensive lunches. It's all tax-deductible.

As long as you're having three square meals.

Absolutely, Mum. I never leave home without breakfast. I don't know when I'll get chance to ring you now. I'm so busy at the moment. I think about you all the time. I'm sorry I've not been in touch.

As long as you're okay, love. That's all that matters.

I'm fine, Mum. I'm doing great. Everything is… Well, it couldn't be better at the moment. Everything is great.

Are you sure? You sound a bit strange.

There was another awkward pause.

Mum?

Yes love.

I … I love you.

I know you do, dear.

Bye.

He switched off his phone. He let the phone drop. It pirouetted through the air. There was some snow – fine flakes – falling now. The weather forecast had been right for a change. The phone hardly made any sound at all when it hit the water below. It had disappeared.

THE BLUE & THE DIM &
THE DARK CLOTHS

She called them flumps. I always thought that was an odd term, 'flump'. When I was a child there was a television programme with the same name. They were a family of furry creatures. I liked the theme tune. I didn't like my mother calling my marshmallow sweets 'flumps', as it made me think of the characters from *The Flumps* television programme rather than something soft and sweet. And I didn't want to think about that as I bit into them. More importantly, the word 'flump' belittled the confectionary, making it silly in my eyes, babyish. In any case, the flump is a particular type of marshmallow and shouldn't be used as a catch-all term for any marshmallow. A flump is specifically a marshmallow twist of both pink and yellow marshmallow. Mother used to buy a bag of Bassett's flumps on a Tuesday after swimming. I liked the ingredients which included – alongside the expected syrup, sugar and cornflower – imagination and unicorn dust.

Haribo do a good range called Chamallows. They come in 150 gram bags for 99p. I generally need five or six bags' worth for a single trip because I can only use half of those, as they are a mix of pink and white marshmallow sweets, and I only use pink marshmallow sweets. I wish I had a use for the white ones, but they usually get thrown in the bin. There's a range called Little Becky marshmallows. They come in a large 280 gram bag and there used to be a variety of pink-only sweets for £1.95 a bag. But they have discontinued the range and you can only purchase white-only packets these days. Which are no use.

Recently, I came across a retailer selling a brand of marshmallows called Frisia. You can buy them in 500 gram bags for £5.75. Again, they are a mix of pink and white marshmallows and the white ones are discarded. I like these as one packet is enough for one outing. I decant the pink ones into a fabric bag which has a decent-size strap so I can carry it over my shoulder easily. These marshmallows are almost pillowy. A very soft pink colour. If you put one between your thumb and index finger and squeeze gently, it is almost like squeezing human flesh. Sometimes I put four or five in the palm of my hand and close my eyes. Then I make a fist, squeezing the soft flesh of the sweet, feeling its softness and malleability through my grip. I squeeze harder until the flesh of the sweet starts to ooze between my fingers.

Saturday morning is the best day and time. About nine o'clock usually, or as soon as the store opens. I try to dress anonymously. My hair is a little longer than average length and is due a cut, but mother always used to cut my hair and I don't like anyone else touching it with their fingers. I generally put it off until there is nothing else for it. I don't want my long hair to draw attention to me though, so I conceal it under a navy-blue Thinsulate hat. I favour large supermarkets that are brightly lit with lots of aisles. The first few aisles are usually too busy and I tend to go for the aisle with canned goods and packets of spices.

I put on my jacket and zip it up to the top. I make sure there are no loose strands of hair poking out of my hat. I check my bag one more time to make sure there are no white ones, then put it over my shoulder. I have three pound coins in my pocket for a large tea and a toasted teacake for afterwards. This is how I like to relax when it's over: on my own in Karin's Kaff sitting in the corner with my newspaper, a steaming mug of tea and a toasted teacake, just like mother's. I pick up my bus pass and my door keys and leave the house.

It's quite chilly out, but it's bright and there's no sign of rain. It's important to have dry conditions; not too hot though, as that can be a disaster. Not every outing is a success; in fact, most end in disappointment, but it is statistically a rare occurrence, so everything has to be just right. I catch a number 36 into town and sit on my own towards the back of the bus, where it's hot from the engine. I worry my bag of marshmallows will get too soft so I move further down where it is cooler. I get off before the bus station and walk up the hill towards Morrisons. I go past the covered market. I've used it once or twice, but I generally find that the floor is too dirty.

There is quite a lot of activity in Morrisons, particularly at the front of the store where all the fresh produce is kept. I make my way to the fifth aisle. I have a full-sized trolley and I've put a few items in it so as not to arouse suspicion – a bunch of bananas, some milk, cheese, cleaning products – but I won't be buying them. I make sure to only walk along the inside of the aisle, keeping as close to the edge as I can. The floor is perfect, so clean and shiny, almost a mirror surface. There are clearly large parts of it that have not been walked on since the floor was polished earlier this morning and the store was opened. I walk past packets of ground all-spice and dried parsley. I stand and examine the packets and jars, pretending to be interested.

I see a mother with a pram. She looks lovely and young but the child, or more accurately, the pram, is a complication. I pick up a jar of smoked paprika and turn it over. I've no idea what it's used for but I like the colour. I put it back and take a box of Shwartz mixed herbs. The aisle is clear when I spot her. She must be in her early twenties. Her hair is naturally blonde. She is wearing a black pencil skirt with a white blouse and a fern-green cardigan. She sways as she walks. She has black shoes on with a two-inch heel. Not too high but still categorically, a stiletto. The thinner the tip the better. I can feel my heart pumping hard in my chest. I take out a marshmallow and hold it gently between my fingers. She approaches without looking at me. I don't want her to look at me. I don't want her to notice anything about me.

I keep still, trying to breathe as calm as I can, but I can feel the blood build inside me and I have to breathe through my mouth to get enough oxygen. She's almost on a level and it's then that I take my chances and without moving my body, manage to flick the sweet onto the floor just before her path. She doesn't notice this, I've got away with it. She walks purposefully, scanning the shelves. She's about to stand on the soft pink flesh. I hold my breath, but then she stops and reaches over to take a tin of chickpeas off the shelf, diverting her direction of travel.

The moment is over. The marshmallow is wasted. I wait for her to pass and then kick it under the shelving unit. I don't want anyone else to have it. I don't want anyone else to stand on it. She's gone.

I linger on my spot. An old couple with one of those tartan shopping contraptions on wheels seem to take forever to make their way down the aisle, eventually taking a tin of value baked beans from the shelf and shuffling off to another aisle. A single man in his forties, on his mobile phone with a plastic shopping basket, has a bottle of wine and a premium-range pizza poking out. He finds a jar of olives and puts it in the basket while continuing his conversation.

I pretend to take interest in a box of curry powder. It's another fifteen or twenty minutes before my next opportunity. A woman in her early twenties. She's wearing tight blue jeans and a leather jacket. Her hair is dark brown. She wears boots with a metal tip, which clink as each foot makes contact with the floor. The spike is just the right size. I feel my pulse begin to rise again. I can feel beads of sweat trickle down my back. My head is too warm in my hat, but it has to stay. This is my moment. She's perhaps fifteen yards away, and she hasn't noticed me. I put my hand into my bag and carefully take out a marshmallow sweet. I conceal it in my closed hand and wait.

I pretend to glance at the jars, packets and boxes, while, with my peripheral vision, I watch her approach. Her skin is so smooth, and her hair is shiny and wavy. I can't smell any perfume on her. I don't like perfume, only the soft sweet aroma of marshmallow. My timing has to be precise, my aim has to be accurate. I only have one chance. I try and keep my cool but I can feel my excitement rising. I try to regulate my breathing but I almost swoon. I hold on to the shelf for support. Come on, I tell myself, you can do this. You can do it.

So close now. A few feet away. Keeping everything apart from my hand rigid, I allow my hand to roll the sweet in front of her path. She hasn't noticed. She's looking along the aisles. The marshmallow stops rolling a few inches before her feet. Please don't turn away from your course, please stay. And she does. And I can hardly believe it as she lifts up her black-booted foot and brings it down on the soft confectionary. The boot is descending. The glint of the steel tip. The sharp point of the heel skewers the pink pillowy sweet. Right through the middle. My timing is perfect, my aim is true. And there it is, the sweet on the end of her stiletto.

She stops. She's noticed it now. She lifts up her foot and sees the sweet skewered there. She bends down and takes the sweet off her heel. No time for hesitation. Quick as a flash, I run across and grab the sweet off her. She is too shocked to stop me. I take it in my fingers and place it in my mouth. It sits on my tongue. I feel the wound with the tip. The rush of saliva secreting is almost painful, my mouth awash with digestive juices. I close my eyes and I tongue the wound again, feeling already the enzymes in my saliva start to dissolve the sugars. I suck this syrup back into my throat. I trap the sweet between my tongue and the roof of my mouth and squeeze. I feel all the juice swill around my gums and the inside of my cheeks. I swallow the mixture down. Then, I take what's left and bite into it. Slowly, gently, savouring every moment of this ecstasy. At first it is firm but soon yields to my bite. I chew and chew and chew, until eventually, reluctantly, I swallow it all down.

I open my eyes. Everything is illuminated, shining gold and silver. I lean against the canned goods and feel the rush of emotion travel down my spine. I take in a deep breath. Then I notice her. The woman sent from heaven for me. She is standing where she was before, staring at me. I want to talk to her, to thank her, to explain how much she means to me, but she looks at me with disgust. With repulsion.

I am a poor man, I can offer you nothing, I want to say. You are a goddess and I am the dirt you walk on. But I have placed my dreams under your feet. I have spread my embroidered cloths. I have spread them for you. Only for you. But I don't say anything and now I am watching her turn her back on me and she's walking down the aisle. Then she's turning the corner and I'm on my own again, amongst the tins and spices.

STORY WITHOUT MEANING

Well, I can see you're not a dick, said God.

I was sitting in the largest of the three dressing rooms, drinking a tin of Tennents with God. He was smartly dressed in a navy-blue suit, a pair of shiny Oxfords and a crisp white open-necked shirt. His hair was medium length and light brown. He was clean shaven. His eyes were a pale blue-grey. He was of medium height with a slightly stooped gait. He looked to be in his mid-fifties, but obviously that was an illusion.

He wasn't what I'd expected exactly. I'd told myself for months to keep an open mind. He wasn't going to fit any stereotype. But for some reason, I'd had this image of Charlton Heston when he played Moses in *The Ten Commandments*. Why Moses? Well, I suppose he looked biblical. Like the god that Michelangelo painted. In fact, the more I considered it, the more the depictions of God I had seen all looked pretty much the same. Stately, noble, long grey hair, beard, nice tan, white smock or bare-chested and rippling with elderly muscle, like a stockier Iggy Pop. But of course these were western depictions. Quite different from Krishna or Buddha or Apocatequil.

Van Eyck's God was a bit more pimped up, with lots of gold and rubies. Del Castagno, Quellin, Michelangelo – they all showed him looking a bit cross. But here he was sitting opposite me, looking quite relaxed. A bit bored, if anything.

He reached into his inside suit pocket and pulled out a packet of Benson and Hedges.

Is it all right to smoke in here?

He looked around the room.

Er, no, sorry, it's not. I pointed to the smoke alarm. I felt a bit foolish telling God not to smoke.

He tapped me on the shoulder.

I hear what you're saying, cocker, he said, and took out a cigarette anyway. He put it in his mouth and lit it with a cheap disposable lighter. So what if the alarm went off, what was front of house going to do? They couldn't exactly throw God out of the building, could they?

So what we gonna talk about? he said.

Well, I thought we could start with Richard Dawkins.

Who?

He's a scientist – written a lot about you not existing.

Oh, right.

He shrugged as though the subject was pointless, which I suppose, now, it was.

I've prepared some questions, I said, but I'd rather it was more like a conversation. I thought we could see how it goes.

Fine by me, he said, and flicked ash on the floor.

I looked up at the alarm. It hadn't gone off. Sign of divine intervention? He took a long drink from his tin.

Listen, he said, come and get me at quarter past seven. We'll have a glass of that champagne.

Then he put the tin down and shooed me off. But it didn't feel discourteous. Just like he was tired and had what he needed. He'd been appraising me, that was all, seeing who I was.

I went out to the front and peeked at the crowd from a gap in the door. The event had sold out almost immediately, months ago now, when I first advertised it. I could have got a bigger venue, charged more for the tickets, but it was daft to think about that now. I'd chosen this venue because I liked the acoustics and because it was nice and light and airy. I wanted the audience to ask questions, and it was important that the space wasn't too intimidating. I'd thought about using the cathedral but the acoustics were a bit echoey. I'd worried that God wouldn't really come across very well, assuming that his voice would be big and booming. But in actual fact it was, if anything, a bit nasally.

The BBC film crew were already in the theatre. I'd sorted

out two boxes for their cameras either side of the stage. Other media companies had offered more money, but I thought it was better that it was the BBC – seemed more appropriate for the occasion. Sky just didn't seem pious enough, nor did Fox.

When I was little and it was time for bed my mum used to tell me a story. It was always me who would get her to tell it.

Tell me about the sexton, I'd say.

You know what a sexton is, don't you? she'd say, and I'd tell her a sexton was someone whose job it was to tend the graves. She knew that I knew the answer, and I knew that she knew that I knew that answer. It didn't matter. It was a ritual. And then she'd tell the story.

Once upon a time, there was a sexton and one day he was tending a grave when a cat walked up to him on its two hind legs. He was wearing big black boots and a hat and he said to the sexton, 'Tell Tom Tiddledum that Tim Toddledum is dead.' Now the sexton was so taken aback to meet a talking cat that he said 'pardon' even though he'd heard everything the cat had said. The cat looked irritated but then said again, 'Tell Tom Tiddledum that Tim Toddledum is dead.' And with that he walked off, leaving the sexton scratching his head. That night the sexton came home from work and was greeted by his wife. He sat at the table and she served him his evening meal. 'So, how was your day?' she said. 'Well, to be honest, a bit strange.' 'Oh really, why's that?' she said. 'Well, I was out in the graveyard tending to a grave when this cat walked up on its two hind legs. It was wearing big black boots and a hat and said, "Tell Tom Tiddledum that Tim Toddledum is dead."' His wife raised her eyebrows and asked the sexton to repeat what he had said, even though she heard him quite correctly the first time. 'Tell Tom Tiddledum that Tim Toddledum is dead.' And as he said this a little louder than the first time, their old cat Tom, who had been sleeping by the hearth, leapt up and said, 'hooray, I'm king of the cats!' and ran off. Old Tom was never seen again.

What does it mean? I'd always ask my mum, but she would just smile at me, kiss me on top of my head and say goodnight. I was sitting in the smallest dressing room on my own, looking over my list of questions. They all seemed rather pointless. He doesn't even know who Dawkins is, so that's the first set of questions out of the equation. The more I looked at the list the more I could feel my heart pound and my mouth go dry. I was dreadfully nervous. Part of me just wanted to ask him, but what does it all mean, God? But it was too naive a question. Too open, unfocussed. How was he supposed to answer that?

I looked at my watch, not long now. The fear had been building since I'd first sent out the press releases. It came in waves. Some days it was unbearable and I'd think about calling the whole thing off, but then a voice would say, don't be stupid, this is going to be the most important moment of your life. I'd been having nightmares, waking up screaming, lying in my own sweat. My wife thought it was a stupid idea, but I knew in the end, that I'd have to do it and that it would be done.

I'd asked other people at first. I tried David Attenborough, Germaine Greer and Morgan Freeman. I wrote to Parkinson and Richard Dimbleby. I thought Will Self might be interested and I contacted him through his agent. Maya Angelou, Bill Clinton, Gore Vidal, Salman Rushdie, Joanna Lumley. They all turned me down. It was too risky. There was too much at stake. Joanna Lumley had wished me luck in her email, she herself was tied up. Then that voice again, you can do it, don't worry about it. You'll be fine. But I didn't feel fine now. I finished off the tin of Tennents. I need another, I thought, and I walked down to the green room. I went over to the fridge and pulled out another can. I prised it open and took a gulp.

Come on, this is it. You can do it, you're King of the Cats. I tried to recall the lyrics to that Eminem song: his palms are sweaty, knees weak, arms heavy… Yep, that just about described it. I tried to take Eminem's advice, to capture the moment and lose yourself in it. I took another gulp. God's rider had surprised me: forty-eight tins of Tennents, two packets of Benson and Hedges and a bottle of champagne. He could knock back the ale, no question about that. No one was going to drink God under the table.

But this was all voodoo. He was just trying to psyche me out. What he wanted from me was to step up to the stage and take him on as an equal adversary. Well, fuck it, I was going to do it. I drank another mouthful of beer then reached for the chilled bottle of champagne. I took two glass flutes and walked towards God's dressing room.

Good evening, ladies and gentlemen, and welcome to this event, which as you know is God in conversation in front of a live audience. Now, I know what a lot of you are thinking, has he turned up? Right?

This got a bit of a laugh and made me relax a little.

Well he has, so don't worry. He's waiting in the wings now and I'll get him out on stage in a minute. Before I do, I'd just like to say a few things. When I invited God to come and talk to me at this event, it was really just a pipedream. I'd talked about it a lot with friends and colleagues and they'd all laughed or said that I was mad. Then one day, I thought, what the hell? Why not? What's the worst that can happen? So I plucked up all the courage I could muster and wrote to him. When I finished the letter, I wasn't sure what to put on the envelope, but in the end just settled for 'God'. I'd had quite a bit to drink, I don't mind admitting, when I posted it later that night. Then I forgot about it. It was such a daft idea. So imagine my delight and surprise a few weeks later when I received a reply.

I could feel the crowd fidget. Better get on with it.

But look, you've not come here to listen to my ramblings. We all know why we are here. He doesn't need any introduction so let's get him on now. Please, put your hands together to welcome on stage … God.

Five minutes into the conversation and things were already starting to fall apart.

Have you ever met the devil? I asked.

Is that the best you can do?

He looked genuinely disappointed at the level of our conversation and I felt dismayed. I'd let him down.

What about Iraq?

What about it?

Why don't you intervene?

He stared at me for a long time. I got an electric jolt right through my body. I felt my internal temperature drop two degrees.

Now don't get clever, sunshine, he said at last.

Shit. This is going terribly. Even worse than I thought it was going to go.

I could feel my palms getting all clammy. I kept wiping them on my trousers. I could hardly swallow, my throat was so dry. I asked him a few more questions, but all I got back was a yes, a no, or a don't know. The crowd were getting restless, agitated. Someone three rows back shouted, this is boring. Someone else in the upper circle shouted, I paid fifty quid for this? I tried to keep a lid on it. I changed the subject.

What had he been doing all these years?

None of your fucking business, he said.

That got a laugh. I was playing stooge now but it wasn't working. I had run out of things to say, or rather I had lost the confidence to ask him anything.

Someone else shouted, my mum's just died of cancer and it's your fault.

Then someone threw a bottle and it just missed my head.

I stood up, angry now. Who threw that?

But it was too dark to make anything out in the audience.

What about the Holocaust? What about Rwanda?

Another bottle.

Then God stood up. I think that's it, he said. And without another word he wandered off.

Backstage I was close to tears. I could hear the crowd shouting. Twenty minutes, that was all I'd managed. And not one answer worth the price of the ticket. Nothing. I couldn't blame them. I had failed completely. What was I thinking about? No wonder Joanna Lumley had wished me luck. I went to the green room and reached into the fridge for a tin of Tennents. There were only a dozen or so left. I drank the lager in huge gulps. Then I heard the dressing room door go. Next the door of the green room opened and in walked God. He nodded acknowledgement then walked over to the fridge. He took out a carrier bag from his suit pocket and filled it up with the remaining tins.

Look, God, I know I made a balls of that, but can I ask you one last thing?

Go ahead.

He closed the fridge door and walked towards the back door exit.

It's just something … I know it's a … well, what I was going to ask is, what does it … what does it all mean?

He'd opened the back door exit and was standing at the threshold. He beckoned me over. As I got close he looked at me and smiled to himself, then shook his head.

You've got a fucking cheek, haven't you…? Listen, he said, you did all right.

He put the bag of beer down. Then he took my head in his hands and kissed me on my forehead.

Relax, don't worry about it, son, he said. Pretty soon it will all be over and then it won't mean anything, again.

He picked up the bag and walked along the corridor leading to the fire exit. I followed him. I wanted to ask him something else. The door closed automatically behind me and we were both in darkness briefly, until God reached the fire escape and pushed the bar which opened the door. For a moment he was lit up in a rectangle of white light, his light brown hair a halo of gold, then he closed the door behind him, leaving me in a long dark corridor with a closed door at either end.

THE BLACK MAN AND
THE WHITE MAN

The black man was stroking his hair and looking at his watch when the white man approached.

Do you mind if I sit here? asked the white man. He pointed to the empty bar stool next to the black man.

Yes I do, said the black man.

What I meant is, is there anyone sitting here?

Well, there is.

But there isn't, though, is there?

What do you want?

To sit here.

Well, you can't.

The white man hovered round the stool.

Do you want some money? The black man reached into his pocket. Here you are – here's a quid. Now piss off.

I don't want a quid. Look see. He emptied his pockets. I've got loads of money. I don't need it. He handed back the coin to the black man. He pulled out the chair and sat down.

Look, I thought I made it clear. I'm not being funny. I don't mind talking to weirdos in pubs normally, but I'm waiting for someone.

I know.

Do you?

Yeah.

How?

You told me.

No I didn't.

You did. Just then. You said, I don't mind talking to weirdos in pubs normally, but I'm waiting for someone. The white man paused before adding: you're waiting for a woman.

How do you know that?

I can just tell. It's obvious really. If you were waiting for a man, you wouldn't keep stroking your hair.

I'm not stroking my hair.

Not now, but you were, before. You were stroking your hair a lot. The white man paused again. I'll tell you what else. You've never met this woman before … I'm right, aren't I?

Look mate, no offence, but if you don't mind… The black man nodded to the chair the white man was sitting in. The white man ignored him.

I'll tell you how I know. First, if you'd met her before, you'd relax a bit more. You've got that feeling here… The white man leaned forward, attempting to touch the black man's stomach but the black man recoiled.

Get off! What you doing?

Sorry, mate, but you're a bit tetchy, aren't you. A bit het up. You want another beer, help you relax a bit?

I'm fine. I don't want another drink.

I'll buy you one.

I don't want one. Now please, it's almost empty in here. There are loads of other places to sit…

I like sitting here. You get a good view of the bar.

Both men sat in silence. The black man looked around the room. He stroked his hair.

You did it again.

Eh?

You stroked your hair.

No I didn't.

You don't know you're doing it. It's weird that, isn't it? The mind and the body. They can do things to each other without the other knowing about it. Weird, isn't it?

The black man ignored the white man.

You see, the other thing, right, is the way you were looking around. You look at every woman as she walks through the

126

door. Not at the men, just the women. And when one walks in, you look at her expectantly, you try and make eye contact, until she walks past you. You're on a blind date. You've never seen her before.

I have seen her, as a matter of fact. So that's where you're wrong.

Photographs don't count, because you can never be sure with a photograph. The hair might have changed – be a different colour. Or she might have had it cut. The thing about a photograph is you never know when it was taken. You never know what time has passed between now and when the photo was taken.

How did you know I'd seen a photograph?

The white man shouted over to the bar, 'scuse me, love. Can we have two more beers? Lager, is it?

I've told you, I don't want one.

Two more lagers over here. Cheers.

What is it with you?

I just guessed.

You what?

About the photograph. Obvious really, isn't it? Most things are when you sit and think about them. You wouldn't have agreed to meet her if you hadn't seen a picture. Blokes are like that. We're very visual. We need to see. With women, well, they don't. Not as much.

Listen, yeah, that's all very interesting, but…

A barmaid brought two pints of lager over to their table. The white man turned to the woman. Cheers, love. He handed her a ten pound note. Keep the change… She put the money in the pocket at the front of her apron and walked back to the bar.

Seven quid for two beers. Crazy, isn't it? Don't you think? Crazy world?

There are enough crazy people in it. The black man nodded to the white man.

Well, no offence taken. It takes one to know one and all that.

You calling me a nutter?

Course not… Well, yeah, I mean we all are. No offence, eh?

The black man ignored the white man. The white man leaned forward and said in a lowered voice, Look. I appreciate your situation. You're waiting for a woman. It's your first date. You want to make the right impression. You don't want her to think you're the sort of bloke who attracts nutters in pubs. It'll make her suspicious. Blokes who attract weirdos in pubs tend to be weirdos, right?

I'm no weirdo.

I understand all that. I'm just having a pint, that's all. I'll drink that, then I'll be off, okay. As soon as she comes, I'll scarper. If a woman comes in, I'll make myself scarce. All right?

I suppose.

The black man looked to the door. The white man looked at the black man.

You come here a lot then?

Now and again.

You've never been in here before.

You what?

It's the first time you've stepped inside this pub.

No, it's not.

I'll tell you how I know.

The black man ignored the white man.

I'll tell you how I can tell… When you walked in, you looked at all the pumps before you ordered. You'd never seen them before.

You been spying on me?

Course not… Well, yeah, a little bit. I mean you do, don't you? When someone walks into a pub, you watch them. Nothing pervy about that, is there? Human nature that's all. We're curious people.

Listen, mate, I'm not being funny, but you're starting to get on my wick. And if you don't stop getting on my wick, I'm gonna land you a punch. You got that?

You're a big bloke.

You what?

One punch from you and I'd be flat out cold.

Well, if you don't watch it, you'll soon find out.

I don't mind.

You what?

I don't mind, you getting violent. It's understandable. You're afraid.

What you say?

You're afraid. People are afraid of what they don't know.

You think I'm afraid of you? I could flatten you like that.

Course you could. You're a big bloke… People are afraid of all sorts of things. High places, small places, open places, insects… You name it.

Now, listen, for the last time, if you don't shut up I'm going to waste you up and down this pub. Got that?

Like I say, no offence.

The black man ignored the white man.

You work out.

Eh?

You work out. You lift weights. You do squats, chin ups, bench press – stuff like that. I can tell.

Well, I do, as a matter of fact.

So you work out?

Yeah.

And does it?

Eh?

Work out?

You what?

Does working out work out..? Sorry, it was just … I was just having a laugh, that's all. No offence, eh?

The white man offered his hand. The black man stared at him but then reluctantly shook the white man's hand.

182 pounds.

You what?

That's what you weigh. 182 pounds.

How the fuck you know that?

That's one of my party tricks, that. The hangman used to do that. When they used to hang people, the hangman used to shake the condemned man's hand. He wasn't being friendly. It wasn't like, how yer doing there fella, nice day for it… From that handshake he could work out his weight.

Why would he want to do that?

He needed to know the weight so that he could calculate the drop. If he got it wrong and he made the drop too long, he'd decapitate the man. It sometimes happened, that. The drop was so long the head came off. And if he made the drop too short, he wouldn't die. He'd just hang there, choking, going purple and kicking his legs about. Wriggling. Like a worm on the end of a line.

Well, that's a good trick. It's impressive. I'm impressed.

Aren't you gonna tell me your name?

No.

I bet I could guess it.

Listen, what do you think this is, Rumpelstiltskin?

I'll call you Killa.

You what?

It's just my term of reference. Jerry Lee Lewis used to call everyone Killa.

The white man attempted a Jerry Lee Lewis impersonation.

Elvis was the greatest, but Jerry Lee Lewis here is the best, Killa. That's what he used to call people, Killa. Even though that was *his* nickname. He never called himself Killa. He always called himself Jerry Lee, or Jerry Lee Lewis.

Did he really?

Yeah. There's a lot of that. In show business. Referring to yourself in the third person. Bit weird, isn't it?

I suppose it is.

He was funny about his name. He came out to greet the press one time. It was this big press conference. I think he'd just shot someone or something. There was a lot of stuff in the paper about him anyway, and he says – the white man attempted his impersonation again – boys, I hear ya'll bin doin' a lot o writing about me and I can't say as ah blame ya. And I want ya'll to know ah don't give a damn what ya write about me, but if one oyous evah spells mah name wrong, ahm gonna find im and come kill is ass…! Funny that, isn't it?

Suppose it is.

But no one ever did.

Eh?

No one ever spelt his name wrong.

Well, they wouldn't, would they? He's a nutcase.

No, but see, you're missing the point. The point is, his name is easy to spell. Everyone can spell Jerry Lee Lewis. Everyone knows Jerry because of Tom and Jerry. It's put into your head from being a kid. And Lee, I mean that's easy. Same with Lewis. So it was really very clever. Because he was making a threat. It sounded like a threat, but he knew no one would ever get it wrong. So it makes him look hard without him actually ever having to carry it out. You see, you think he's a nutter, and in some ways he is, but he's also very clever. Like with the Elvis thing. Elvis was the greatest, but I'm the best. Again, it's a clever put-down. Cos you can be great in lots of ways. A mountain can be great, or a bird can be great. A great crested grebe. A great skua. A great snipe. A great tit…

All right. I get the idea.

I knew a great tit once. Right arsehole… You get it?

Yes. I see.

Knew a great tit, right arsehole. The white man laughed to himself. Or a war. They talk about the Great War. They don't mean it was really good, do they? It just means big. And Elvis was big, wasn't he? A big fat man. And Jerry wasn't. He was small and wiry… But you see, best just means best. If you're the best, you're the best, you can't get any better.

You remind me of someone.

Do I?

This girl I'm supposed to meet. She talks like that. She knows loads about music. Really into it.

Are you?

Yeah. Yeah, I like my music, but I don't have a head like that. I mean I don't remember stuff. I do a lot of reading. I like reading, but I don't keep it in here.

The black man tapped his head with his right index finger.

Like you do. And like she does.

You sound like you're keen.

I am.

Is it serious?

Yeah, I suppose it is.

She likes you. A lot.

How do you know that?

Stands to reason. Why would she arrange to meet you if she wasn't really keen on you?

Well, I suppose. But the thing is. She hasn't.

How do you mean?

She was supposed to be here half an hour ago. That's a long time to keep someone waiting. If she thought a lot about me she'd have turned up on time.

You don't know that.

I knew it was a mistake. It's always the way when I… Well, you know, when you like someone.

When *you* like someone or when *I* like someone?

Eh?

You said, when you like someone, meaning me.

I best go. She's not coming now.

How did you meet her?

Chatroom. You know, on the internet.

Yes, I know what you mean.

You use them?

Yeah. It's the best way to get to know someone. You know when you meet someone, you look at them and you judge them. It only takes a few seconds. You judge them entirely on their physical appearance. Like with me, yeah. You took one look at me and thought, headcase, right?

Well, y'know, when people approach you in pubs…

Don't feel you have to apologise. It's the most natural thing in the world. Everyone does it. Dogs sniff each other's arses. One sniff and they decide straightaway whether they like each other or not. One sniff, one look, it's the same snap judgement.

Well, yeah, I suppose.

But with the chatrooms, you bypass all that. It's like you're tapping directly into someone's head. It's like a portal straight into their skull. It's the most truthful, most intimate, most meaningful form of communication. You fall in love with someone in a chatroom, and you've fallen in love with *them*. Not what they look like, not what they wear, but what's inside. Right inside them. The real person.

Do you think so?

I know so.

But I don't get it. If she was so keen to see me, she'd be here, right?

She would. Or she'd find a way of getting hold of you.

Well, she's got my mobile number. I mean, she'd ring.

She hasn't got a phone.

How do you know?

Just suppose.

There's always a call box.

Is there?

Course.

Have you tried using a call box lately…? It's a fucking nightmare. You've got to find one first of all. Then you've got to try and find one that accepts coins. You try and find one someone hasn't shat in. You try and find one that hasn't got hypodermic needles scattered on the floor. You eventually track one down, right, and you go in it and it stinks of piss or stale spunk, and you get your money out and you put it in and the headset is all greasy and dirty and you put your money in and nothing… It doesn't work. It's fucked.

She hasn't got a mobile.

There you go.

She doesn't like using phones. I tried to get her to call me. I tried to call her. She said she wanted to meet me in person.

That's because she likes you.

You think so?

Course it is. She wouldn't want to meet you in the flesh if she wasn't interested.

She would have phoned you first.

Listen, it was nice talking to you. I mean, you're a bit of a weirdo, but, you know, an interesting one… She isn't going to turn up now. I'm going.

The black man stood up.

Wait. You're right. She isn't coming.

How do you know?

She told me.

She told you?

She told me she couldn't make it. Susan told me that something had come up.

She's really sorry. She's really very sorry.

You know Susan?

Sit down.

The black man did as he was told.

I'm her brother.

You what?

I'm her twin brother.

What?! I mean, why? Why wouldn't you just say? What's this all about?

Look, I'm sorry. She's got a sense of humour. You know that. She likes a joke.

I don't call standing someone up a joke.

Look, she genuinely regrets not being here today. She had to go to my dad. He's ill and he wanted to see her. She couldn't get out of it. She tried everything. I told her I'd go in her place, but he wanted to see her. It meant something to him. You understand? I'm really sorry. I'm really sorry I pulled this stunt. It was just a joke at first, but I wanted to find out.

Find out what? I've told her everything about me.

I know. I'm sorry. She thinks the world of you. She insisted I came to explain. This was all my idea. This wind-up, I mean. Stupid idea. But I wanted to know what you were made of. I wanted to know if you were good enough… I can't help it. I look after her. I always have. We're twins, but I was born first. There's something there, psychological. I've always looked after her. Susan… She's a bit special. She's not like other girls. She's something different. Better. She… Well, I wanted to make sure you were right for her.

And?

I can see you are. But you shouldn't have doubted her.

That was a dirty trick you played.

Look, I've said I'm sorry. I know. I shouldn't have done it. But I needed to know. I needed to test you. If you were Susan's twin brother, you'd have done the same. Do you see that now?

Perhaps… Look, you've seen me now. Tell her I'll email her. Tell her I'm sorry she didn't make it.

I will. Don't worry. I'll tell her how much you wanted to see her… Look, you're here now, why not have another beer?

I best get off. I mean, what's the point?

The white man shouted over to the bar. Excuse me… Two more beers, please.

The black man stood up. I'm going. Don't get one for me.

Please. Just stay for one. I'd appreciate that. Susan would appreciate it. I'll tell you things about her.

The black man put his hand on the back of his chair.

Somehow, half an hour had passed and the black man had still not left. The white man was still talking.

He said that Sid on bass, right, displayed all the dexterity of a one-legged man at an arse-kicking contest.

135

The black man laughed. I like that, I've heard it before. A one-legged man at an arse-kicking contest. It's good that. I'll try and remember it.

But you won't.

How do you know?

You don't remember things.

Course I do. Just because I'm not a geek like you.

Like her.

Heh, listen, Susan's not a geek.

Susan's like me.

There's a family resemblance. I can see that. But you're really quite different.

If Susan was a bloke, she'd be me.

Yeah, right.

And if I was a girl, I'd be Susan.

Not necessarily. I mean, I've got a sister, we're the same star sign and everything. She was born two years after me, three days before my birthday. But we've got nothing in common.

Susan told you that.

Told me what?

About Sid Vicious.

Yeah, well, she might have done. We talk a lot about music because we're both into punk, and she gets fed up because people her age don't know the roots. They don't know the history. They think it starts with Green Day… And we do, see, we listen to the lot, right back to the Stooges. It's just one of the things we've got in common.

We've got in common. The thing about Sid Vicious though, it's interesting this.

I know all about it. I've got loads of video stuff. And books. I've read loads of books on it.

This is something you don't know. Something Susan didn't tell you. And you won't have read it in a book.

Go on.

You know how he died, don't you?

Course I do. He was smacked out. Took a drug overdose.

136

That's right. He got arrested for killing Nancy.

I know, he stabbed her, then he rang the police.

Right. And he got banged up, but Malcolm McLaren put up the bail and he got out a few days later.

I never understood that.

What?

How he got released.

That's just the American legal system. I don't understand it either. I mean OJ Simpson, right – how did he get off? Same difference… Anyway, they let him out on bail, but one of the conditions of his bail was that he wasn't to take any drugs or even approach a dealer … and his mum knew that. She also knew that the first thing he would do was score some smack. Well, maybe not the first thing, but as soon as he got withdrawal symptoms he'd be there like a shot. And then he'd be in jail again for violation of his bail conditions, right.

Yeah, I read something about that.

What you won't have read is that it was his mum, you see, who scored the smack. She'd never done it before. She didn't know any dealers. But she managed to get hold of some. Only, unlike the crap he'd been scoring, cut with all sorts, this stuff was pure. In her ignorance, she'd managed to score some completely uncut heroin.

I get it. So that's what killed him? Because he wasn't used to it pure. Is that it?

Yeah, that's it. He injected the usual amount, right. But of course it wasn't the usual amount. It was a lot more.

So Sid's mum killed Sid… Wow.

In trying to save Sid. In trying to stop him going back to prison, she killed him. She killed her own son. Each man kills the thing he loves. Or in this case, each woman.

I've heard that.

Oscar Wilde.

That's right. Either with a sword or with a word, isn't it?

Yeah. Thing is, do you believe it?

Believe what?

Do you believe each man kills the thing he loves?

I don't know really. Well, I suppose the way I understand it, it doesn't have to be literal. It's part of growing up. The things you love as a kid. Say music. I was always in bands, but in order to, you know, in order to live, I had to ditch it.

Why did you have to ditch it? I don't understand.

I was in this punk band. A bit like the White Stripes. Only we were a bit more out there. You know, the lyrics were a bit weirder, but the music was really stripped down. Punk and blues. That was our main influence. And grunge bands.

You like Nirvana, don't you?

Yeah, I suppose Susan told you that. We're both big Nirvana fans.

Me too.

Is that right? They were great, weren't they?

They were more than great. They were gods. Well Kurt Cobain anyway. I wasn't too struck on the others.

Kurt Cobain, yeah, that's what I meant.

He sacrificed himself.

Well…

So you don't have to.

Well, I don't quite see it that way myself. The way I see it, it was… Well, it didn't have to happen. I blame Courtney Love. She was like Nancy was to Sid. She was a leech. She was bad news from the start.

Say what you were going to say.

About what?

About killing the thing you love.

Oh yeah, right. Well, we were in this band, see. I was the singer, and I played bass. We were really good. Well, everyone thinks they're really good, but you know, we were. Lots of people told us. Julian Cope came to one of our gigs. He's a bit of a hero of mine. He came up to us after the gig and told us we had talent.

That's really something. You must have been exceptional.

Well, like I say, we were good. We brought an album out.

Did it ourselves. Burnt the CDs ourselves. We used to sell them at the gigs. But we couldn't get a record contract. It was mad. We had a really strong following, you see. And the CDs used to sell at every performance. But we could never get a record deal. We had a few A and

R men check us out. We kept telling each other it was only a matter of time.

How long did this go on for?

A couple of years. Not that long really. But you see, I couldn't take it. I knew we should be up there. Being reviewed in the *NME* and all that. Playing all the festivals. I couldn't stand not being where we deserved to be. It was eating me up. I was so down all the time. I mean really down. I used to have really bad thoughts.

What kind of thoughts?

Well, you know about Charles Manson?

Yeah, I know about him all right. You can't be into grunge and punk and all that and not know about Charles Manson.

Well, I reckon that's why he did all the things he did. You know, got all those hippies to kill Sharon Tate and all those other people. It was because of the rejection.

Charles Manson would have been a great rock star. The best. He had the charisma, and he had the talent.

Totally. I mean, he had a really versatile voice, and he was a great musician, and he was a complete one-off.

Unique.

And if we lived in a fair world…

But we don't.

No.

And you think you'd be like him? Like Charles Manson?

I was. I mean, I was getting there. I've never told anyone this, but there was one time…

Go on.

I've drank too much.

You've not drank enough.

It's not that I don't trust you.

What then?

It's hard to admit it.

You thought about killing someone.

I'd rather not talk about it.

You thought if you killed that one person, then nothing could stand in your way.

Something like that.

You thought if you broke the last social taboo, you'd be invincible. More than invincible, you'd be a god, because only a god has the ability to take a life away. Isn't that right?

I was insane. I mean, I realised almost straight away…

How close did you get?

Close.

How close?

Well, let's just say, I was saved by the bell … and it made me think later, about

Charles Manson.

What about him?

Well, where Roman Polanski and Sharon Tate lived … I forget what it was called.

One-hundred-five-oh Cielo Drive.

Yeah. Well it was owned by, this bloke, Doris Day's son.

Terry Melcher he was called.

You know a lot about it.

So do you.

Well, he was going to record Manson, for music for a film.

But he turned him down.

Yeah. Manson thought he was going to strike a deal. He really believed he'd made it. Melcher came to visit him at the ranch several times.

And you think that's why he sent his family to 10050 Cielo Drive?

Well yeah, I mean, people who've made it don't go around killing people, do they?

You'd be surprised.

Probably not.

Do you think you could?

What?

Kill someone.

The black man drank his beer.

I need a leak. Where are the bogs in this place?

Round the other side of the bar.

Listen, I'll get us another drink on the way back. Same again?

You sure? Thought you were heading back.

I'm all right for a bit. I'm getting into this.

Fine. I'll have another lager. Listen, I'll be in that side room over there.

What's wrong with where we are?

Nothing. Only it's getting a bit busy and, well, people hearing us talking about

Charles Manson and that, they might think we're a bit … you know … weird. You know how narrow-minded people are.

Suppose you're right. I'll meet you in there then.

The black man went to the gents. The white man retired to the side room. He found somewhere for them to sit. The black man returned with another round.

It's getting busy. Took me ages to get served. He looked around the room. Quiet in here though. Looks like we're on our own. He handed the white man his drink.

Cheers. Looks that way. Do you mind?

Mind what?

Being on your own. With me.

Don't be daft.

I thought, you know, you thinking I'm a weirdo and that…

Hey, look, I said I thought you were a weirdo when I first met you, that's all.

So you don't think I'm a weirdo now?

Only in the sense that we're all weirdos. I mean, everyone is, once you get to know them.

Don't you think you're different to everyone else then?

Well, I mean, we're all different. From each other, I mean.

Course we are. Only some are more different. Do you see what I'm saying?

Suppose.

You're different.

Do you think so?

I know so.

In what way?

In the way that I'm different.

What makes you say that?

It's something Susan said.

What did she say?

When I was hurting her.

You what?

When I was hurting her, she said something about you. Something you'd told her.

What do you mean, you were hurting her?

Only joking.

Only joking? You don't joke about something like that. Did you hurt her or not?

Not.

Then why say you did?

Well, you know, just testing you again.

Don't do that. Don't do that again. Do you understand me?

Okay, okay, don't get serious. I thought we were having a laugh.

We were. We are. Only, don't say stuff like that. Not even in a joke. I care very deeply for Susan. I don't know what I'd do if I found out anyone had hurt her.

Sorry. I shouldn't have. You're right. Only, when I said it, what did you feel? How did it make you feel inside?

I got a shot of adrenalin. For a second my mind turned over. I felt sick.

That's because you love her so much. You love her so much

that it's unbearable. Sometimes you can't bear the feeling and you wonder whether you're ill. You think you need help. You think you need someone to calm it all down.

I suppose you're right … I don't want to talk about it. What were you talking about before?

About you being different?

Did you mean it, or was that another of your jokes?

I don't joke about stuff like that. You're not someone I'd make a joke about. Do you see that?

I don't know.

You're still not sure about me, are you?

Well, I mean, it's difficult. I've only known you for an hour.

You've known me a lot longer than that. A lot longer than that.

How do you mean?

What I mean is, that the time you say you have known me for and the actual time you have known me for are two very different things.

I know that. I meant, what do you mean about me knowing you a lot longer?

Precisely that. That's all I meant. What I said is what I meant. Sometimes people do that. Sometimes people say what they mean. Not very often, I'll grant you. But from time to time it happens. By chance more than design. But it happens.

Quit messing about.

Look, it's late. That's all I'm saying. I've been here two and a half hours. We've been together nearly two hours now. That's all I'm saying. You thought we'd been together an hour. In actual fact, it's nearly two. See. It's practically double. It's practically double the length of time you *thought* we'd been together. It's funny, that's all. It just goes to show.

Goes to show what?

That you, that we, that our time together today. Well, I mean, it's flown by, hasn't it? Seems only a few minutes ago that I was introducing myself to you. You wouldn't believe it was two hours ago, would you? I mean it was, look. The white man showed the black man his watch. But you'd never guess. You'd have to see the evidence before you'd accept it, right?

What did Susan say about me?

Susan says lots of things about you. Between me and Susan, it's an open book. We don't have secrets, me and Susan. We share everything. Always have done.

What you were saying before. You said it was something Susan said.

Oh that!

What was it?

She was telling me about your career as an athlete.

I'd hardly call it that.

Well, you were a gold medal winner, weren't you?

Only at school. Between other schools, I mean. That's when I won the medals.

That's some achievement.

Not really. I mean, I've always been able to run fast.

Bet it comes in handy, eh!

How do you mean?

Well, you know, it's handy if you can run fast. If you're late for the bus, for instance.

I don't use buses. I've got a car.

Well, let's say you were being chased.

I'd rather stand and fight. I'm not someone who runs away.

I'm not saying you are. But if you were ever to be chased…

It wouldn't happen. I'd stand my ground.

Okay then. You'd stand your ground. But let's say, for some reason, you had to chase someone else. You were the one doing the chasing.

That's possible, I suppose.

There you go then.

You've got a point there, I'll accept that.

There you go. I'm not wrong, am I?

No, you're not wrong.

The black man drank his beer.

You're a bit tetchy sometimes. Do you know that?

I'm sorry. I'm not really a drinker. It makes me aggressive, I suppose. That's why I don't usually drink. I prefer to smoke dope.

Course you do. You do right. You don't see dope smokers out on a Friday night, kicking ten shades of shite out of each other, do you?

I used to get … well, let's just say it doesn't agree with me.

How did you used to get?

I got into a few fights. I used to black out. To tell you the truth I can't remember much about it now.

Well you wouldn't, would you? If you blacked out. Stands to reason. If you black out you black out. Am I right?

Suppose.

There you go … but you remember some of it, don't you?

Er…

Some things you remember quite clearly, don't you? Like it was yesterday. Like it was two hours ago. You close your eyes and you're there. Right?

Some things I remember, that's true. But most of it's a blur.

One incident in particular. You remember one particular incident, don't you?

There was one time…

You remember the rage, don't you? The anger building up inside you, filling you up, right up … so that there was no room for it any more, it had to spill out.

It was an isolated incident. I'm not proud of it.

Tell me about it. I'm a good listener.

I'd rather not. No offence. It's not that I don't trust you, just that…

You're afraid if you tell me, it might happen again. That the act of remembering it is also an act of resurrection. You don't want to resurrect the past, do you?

I don't, no.

But you won't. You've put all this armour up, because you're afraid.

Don't start that again.

Hear me out… That's what all the weightlifting's about. You feel vulnerable. It's okay, we all do. I do. Everyone does. It's perfectly natural. But you can't stand to feel vulnerable. It fills you with self-loathing and this wretched feeling. You can't describe it, but it's like you want to rip yourself out of your own skin.

Yeah, yeah, yeah. That's it. That's right.

It's okay. Relax. It's okay to feel like that … listen to me … look at me … look me in the eye. The black man looked the white man in the eye. Can you see my eyes?

Yes.

They're not hiding anything. Can you see that?

Yes.

There's nothing guarding them. There's nothing protecting them. Can you see that?

Yes, I can see that.

Good. That's good that you can see that.

Those eyes.

What about them?

Well, I mean, you're younger than me. But your eyes, they seem older.

They're stronger, and that makes them seem older. Now listen to me. Listen to what I'm saying. Your vulnerability is your strength. It's only when you admit your weaknesses to others that you become strong inside. A snail's not strong inside, that's why it hides in its shell. Inside, it's soft. And it thinks it can hide beneath that hard exterior. But it can't. All that hard exterior does is advertise its vulnerability. You think if you build up your muscles, if you make yourself bigger and stronger, people will think you're tough. Some people will, I grant you. But those who want to hurt you, they know. They see you and they know that, inside, you're soft…

The white man stared at the black man.

I slept in the dark, in the silent night. I spoke my fear, and I felt delight.

The black man drank his beer.

It's nothing really. I mean, it could have happened to anyone.

Course it could.

He was called Darren. I'd known him since I was four. We'd grown up together. But we used to have these arguments. Sometimes they'd turn into fights. It's weird, because he was my best friend, but there was no one who could get me angrier than him.

That's understandable. That happens.

I can't even remember what we were talking about. We'd had a lot to drink.

You were young. You didn't know your limit.

I just know it turned into an argument. He was red in the face. I can see it now. His face screaming at me. Red with rage. Bits of spit flying out of his mouth. In my peripheral vision, I could make his hands and arms out. He was waving them about. He was shouting so loud, and it was a really busy pub. He was shouting at the top of his voice, and his face was right in my face. I could hardly focus on him, he was so close. And I could feel my own anger boiling up.

And what happened?

I must have blacked out. I just remember coming round. My face felt wet and cold and I didn't know why. Then I saw that someone had thrown a drink in my face. I was on the floor. I had my hands round Darren's throat. His face was purple now. Only not with anger. His eyes were pleading with me. He couldn't breathe. He was choking, and his eyes were popping out. Desperate eyes. Eyes that were pleading with me to stop. There was a crowd of people. I remember their faces. Scared faces. The women in particular. Such looks of shock and disbelief. There were men grabbing hold of me, pulling me off. It took four of them to get me off him. And I felt so …

What did you feel?

I felt so … sick.

Why? Why did you feel sick?

I felt … I felt … weak. I was weak. I was dangerous. I couldn't control myself. I couldn't trust myself.

You were afraid you didn't know who you were. That's what you were afraid of.

Yes.

And you were afraid that if you didn't know, you wouldn't be able to prevent it from happening again.

Yes, I was.

You were afraid of a stranger. And the stranger was you, wasn't it?

Yes. Yes. That's right.

The black man drank his beer.

And your friend? What happened to him?

That was the thing. He didn't seem to hold it against me. He forgave me. Only…

Only, *you* didn't forgive you, did you?

No, I couldn't. I'd nearly killed him. How could I?

So what did you do?

It wasn't a conscious decision. But we drifted apart. It was me that did the drifting. Not him. He tried to keep in contact. But I didn't.

He was a mirror. And when you looked into him, you didn't like what you saw.

No, I didn't.

What you saw was a version of you that you didn't like.

Yes.

And you thought that this might be the true reflection. The real you inside.

Yes.

It's okay. It's okay. I'm going to get us another drink. You'll feel better now.

Thank you.

Here's to friendship. The white man raised his glass and

they chinked. You've lost one friend and that's tragic. But you've found another.

I have?

Course you have. Me.

Oh, I see. That's nice of you.

It's quality not quantity. I mean you can know someone for years and not know anything about them. I mean, what do people want inside? What motivates them?

What makes them laugh? What makes them cry? We never really know. But then take us.

Me and you?

Yeah, me and you. We've only known each other for what? About three hours?

Yeah, about that.

But I bet we know more about each other now than folks who've been friends for years.

I suppose you're right.

Course I am… You know, I feel like I've known you all my life.

Really?

Really.

But you know more about me than I know about you.

That's true. Tell you what, ask me a question. Any question you like.

What did Susan say about me?

When?

Before, you said that Susan said something about me, and then you started talking about my running.

Oh that! Right… It was just something she told me. Don't take it the wrong way.

She wasn't betraying your confidence, you understand that? Me and Susan, we've always told each other everything. You realise that?

Yes. Of course. I won't be hurt.

You won't think bad of Susan.

Not at all.

Won't … won't lose your trust in her?

Certainly not.

She was telling me about that last race you ran.

Oh I see, that.

She was telling me that you were running the one thousand metres and that you were well in the lead. All your school was there supporting you. You were clearly in the lead and it meant a lot for your school. Your triumph was their triumph. You winning would make them all feel good, make them all winners … and then, just as you reached the last leg, you were about ten yards from the finishing line, and you stopped. You stopped in your tracks and you sat down.

Yes.

I admire you for that.

Why?

It took a lot of bottle.

I let people down.

To thine own self be true.

I was weak.

No. You were strong. Don't you see, that when you did that, you stopped doing what other people wanted you to do. And you started being yourself. Most people go through their entire life without reaching that point.

I suppose you're right.

You know I'm right. You have to do what's inside you. Sooner murder an infant in its cradle than *nurse* unacted desire.

Eh?

Sooner murder an infant in its cradle than *nurse* unacted desire.

But isn't that a bit dangerous?

How?

Well, what if what you want to do is bad?

What's bad is not doing what you want to do. What you need to do, to be true to yourself. Bad people are people who haven't done what they needed to do. They've bottled it up. They've distilled all those feelings and created this noxious, rancid poison.

I stopped and I sat down because I didn't want to be a winner any more. I wasn't a winner. I didn't feel like a winner. I wanted to stop pretending.

That's what Susan said.

I didn't tell Susan that.

No, but Susan knew.

The black man drank his beer.

This is nice.

What?

This. Me and you.

Oh, I see… Is Susan all right?

What do you mean?

I'm a bit worried about her.

Well don't be. Susan's Susan. She'll be fine as long as she knows you're with me.

You sure?

Look, I know Susan… Do you trust me?

Er … well, I don't really know you.

No, but do you trust me?

No.

Why?

It's not that I don't trust you, it's just that I've just not had chance to … you know, get to know you.

I trust you.

Why?

I've had chance to get to know you. I know you.

How can you say that?

If you were never to see me again, if this was it, your one and only contact … how would you feel about that?

That's a funny question.

I'm not laughing.

I don't know how to answer it.

You're never going to see me again.

How do you know that? You can't possibly know that.

I'm going away.

But you'll come back.

I'm not coming back.

Maybe not. But you will, eventually. I mean, everyone returns to their roots at some point.

There's something I've not told you about me.

I'm sure there is.

I'm not like you.

Why would you be?

I'm not like you in one significant detail.

What's that then?

Are you a prejudiced man?

What do you mean?

Would you, if you had the power to do so, persecute those who were different from you?

Of course not.

The white man lowered his voice. I'm bent.

Do you mean you're gay?

I'm not gay. I'm bent.

What's the difference?

Gay would imply I was carefree. So you see, I can't be gay.

Why are you telling me this?

The white man closed his eyes. He nodded to himself, then he opened his eyes again. Because I'm in love with you.

What?!

Ever since Susan found you. It was instant.

Don't be ridiculous.

Me and Susan, we've fought a lot about this.

Is Susan all right?

Not really.

Well, is she or isn't she?

Isn't.

What's wrong?

We had a fight about you.

Is she hurt?

Not as such.

The black man stood up. What have you done to her?

Look, please, sit down and I'll explain.

Not till you tell me what you've done to her.

It's a long story.

The black man grabbed hold of the white man. So start talking.

Please. Let go, and I'll tell you.

The black man let go.

Sit down.

The black man sat down.

You've got to understand, before I begin, that I didn't mean to hurt her.

Oh my god! What the fuck have you done?

It was last night.

Last night?!

She'd been hiding your emails. I knew she'd received them. I can always tell. Her eyes light up. But she denied it. She copied them into a folder, then deleted them from the inbox. But I found them. I found out about her meeting you here today and I asked her if I could come with her.

Obviously she'd say no.

I told her it was to protect her. She hates me playing big brother. But the real reason was that I had to see you. Even more than she had to see you. I had to come here and see you for myself. And she knew.

What've you done?

We had an argument. I told her I was going to follow her. I told her she couldn't stop me from seeing you.

Where is she now?

We argued and argued. In the end she got some rope to tie me up. Can you believe that? She threatened to tie me up. I said, don't be ridiculous, I'm not going to let you tie me up. She said she'd wait until I was asleep and tie me to the bed.

Tell me what you've done.

It was late. Neither of us wanted to go to bed first. In the end, I went up. But I couldn't sleep. I knew she'd do it. I got a knife…

Oh fuck! Oh fuck!

I hid it under the pillow and pretended to be asleep. It was about an hour later when she crept into my room. I kept my eyes shut … you must realise that I didn't mean to do it…

This is serious. You've got to tell me exactly what happened.

She started to tie the rope around me. I thought she was near my feet. I did. I thought I could feel her near my feet. I was afraid. I was afraid she had already secured me to the bed. So I leapt up with all my strength. I leapt up with the knife in my hand. I just meant to scare her, I promise you, I just meant to scare her.

The black man grabbed hold of the white man. What've you done?! Where is she? Tell me where she is.

It's too late. She's dead.

The black man paced the room. Oh my god! Oh my god! I don't believe it. I don't believe it.

It was an accident. I promise you.

You've killed her? You've killed Susan?!

Please forgive me. Please forgive me. I didn't know what I was doing. It was dark. It was so dark. It was such a dark … and there was no light. There was no light anywhere. Please. I need your forgiveness.

You've really killed her? I don't believe it. Have you really killed her?

The white man opened his jacket and took out a knife. Here.

The black man picked it up. What's this?

That's the knife.

Oh no! You have, haven't you. You've done it. You've really done it.

I held it like you're holding it now.

What were you doing with this knife? What were you thinking of?

You. I was thinking of you.

This is fucked. You need help.

Will you help me?

ME?! Are you having a laugh. You've just killed Susan. I should…

What should you do?

I don't know. I can't think. My head's fucked… You're having me on. You must be. She's not really dead, is she? Tell me she's not dead. Tell me this is one of your sick jokes.

The white man moved closer. It's not a joke. She's dead, and do you know what?

What?

She didn't come into my room. I lied to you.

The black man grabbed hold of the white man and threatened him with the knife.

You better start telling the truth. You better tell me the fucking truth. You got it?

I went into her room. She was sleeping, and I took the rope and I tied her up…

Tell me what happened!

She woke up. Only I'd tied her good. She started to scream. I wanted her to shut up. I thought she might wake someone. So I stuck the knife in. I used the knife… I held it in her for a long time. I could feel the warmth oozing out. I was covered in her blood. I was seeped in it.

The black man pressed the knife hard against the white man's flesh. You sick bastard!

That feels … nice. I bet that's what … Susan felt only … more so. The white man pushed his chest against the knife, pushing himself onto the knife. That's … nice. That's … it. That's the one.

You sick bastard. You deserve that. You fucking deserve it!

Tonight … I'm going to be … Susan.

What?

I'm … Susan.

What are you talking about?!

I'm … Sue … a boy named … Sue. My dad you see … he was a … Johnny Cash fan, it was a bit of a … joke really. My

155

middle name is … Sue.

What do you mean?

There never was a … Susan. All those … emails. It was … me.

He pushed himself fully onto the knife.

Thank you.

The black man looked aghast. The white man pulled himself off the knife.

I forgive you.

The white man fell onto the floor. He was dead. The black man stared in disbelief. He dropped the knife on the carpet. He thought about picking it up again, but all he could see was the red on the blade. He stood over the body for a long time, before moving out of the side room and into the main bar. He looked around. It was busy now but no one seemed to notice him. It was as if he wasn't there. He walked out of the front of the building and along the street that had been lit by the sun when he'd arrived, but was now womb-red. He looked around at the people spilling in and out of bars. Not one of them knew who he was.

ACKNOWLEDGEMENTS

'The League' was first published as 'The Bald Men' in *Tears in the Fence* issue 49; 'You Are Going Back', *Tears in the Fence* issue 48; 'Mr Jolly', *The Reader Magazine* no. 50; 'The Man In The White Coat', *Riptide Journal* vol. 8; 'Third Person' in *The Light That Remains and other stories* (Leaf Books); 'Above And Beneath' published as 'Monkeys', *Brand Magazine* issue 4; 'The Phone Call', *The Aesthetica Creative Works Annual 2009*; 'The Blue & The Dim & The Dark Cloths', Galley Beggar Press (e-book, 2013); 'Story Without Meaning', *We're Creme De La Crem 2010* (Biscuit Publishing) and subsequently published as an e-book 'single' by Galley Beggar Press in 2015. Many thanks to these publications and publishers.

Big thanks to Jamie McGarry and everyone at Valley Press and also a big thanks to all those who helped with the book at different stages. They are, in no particular order: Simon Crump, Sam Jordison, Jim Greenhalf, Steve Ely, Jessica Malay, Sarah Falcus, Ailsa Cox, Jenn Ashworth, Jonathan Taylor and Nicholas Royle.